Still Yours (Maybe)

She thought she was free to move on...
until the truth brought her
back to where love first began.

Also by Kathryn Kaleigh

The Gravity of Us Series

(Reading Order)

Just Breathe

Just Surface

Just Melt

Standalone Suspense

Out of Ashes

CONTEMPORARY

Alpine Falls (Maybe Yours) Series

(Reading Order)

Still Yours (Maybe)

Yours for Christmas (Maybe)

Forever Yours (Maybe)

(ALPINE FALLS)

Stranded in Alpine Falls

Belonging in Alpine Falls

The Spirit of Christmas in Alpine Falls

Christmas Wishes in Alpine Falls

Finding True North in Alpine Falls

A Ghost of Christmas Magic in Alpine Falls

Secrets and Second Chances

Honeymoon with a Stranger

Not Our Wedding

(SILVER PINES)

The Way Back to You

Back to Where We Began

When We Were Us

(ONCE UPON FOREVER)

My Forever Guy

Our Forever Love

Forever Vows

Finding Forever

Accidentally Forever

(TRUE NORTH)

Borrowed Until Monday

Still Mine

The Moon and the Stars at Christmas

Perfectly Mismatched

On the Way to Forever

A Merry Little Christmas

On the Way Home to Christmas

It was Always You

(UNBREAK MY HEART)

Begin Again

Love Again

Falling Again

(FOR THE LOVE OF THE FLIGHT)

Just Stay

Just Chance

Just Believe

Just Us

Just Once

Just Happened

Just Maybe

Just Pretend

Just Because

(MAGNETIC NORTH)

Second Chance Kisses

Second Chance Secrets

First Time Charm

Three Broken Rules

Second Chance Destiny

Unexpected Vows

(FALLING FOR CHRISTMAS)

The Heart of Christmas

The Magic of Christmas

In a One Horse Open Sleigh

A Secret Royal Christmas

An Old Fashioned Christmas

(CITY SKYLINE BILLIONAIRES)

Billionaire's Unexpected Landing

Billionaire's Accidental Girlfriend

Billionaire's Fallen Angel

Billionaire's Secret Crush

Billionaire's Barefoot Bride

(TRULY, MADLY, DEEPLY)

The Lady in the Red Dress

On the Edge of Chance

Sealed with a Kiss

Kiss Me at Midnight

The Heart Knows

(STOLEN ECHOES)

When Cupid's Arrow Strikes

Chasing Fireflies

A Chance Encounter

(EDGE OF THE HORIZON)

The Forever Equation

Pretend Boyfriend

All our Tomorrows

Kissing for Keeps

Out of the Blue

The Princess and the Playboy

(RED LIPSTICK KISSES)

Red Lipstick Kisses and Small Town Wishes

Stolen Dances and Big City Chances

Chance Connections and Upside Down Plans

A Christmas Kiss on the Twenty-Fifth

Believe in the Magic of Christmas

Vows of Inheritance Series

(Reading Order)

Vow to Protect

Vow to Redeem

Scripted in the Stars

Destined in the Twilight

Promised in the Mist

Trapped in the Melody

(DRAGON'S BLOOD)

Dragon's Blood

Lavender Blue

Champagne Silver

Twilight Frost

Mountbatten Pink

(WHEN HEARTSTRINGS BECKON)

Rescued in Time

Meet me in 1879

(WHEN HEARTSTRINGS ECHO)

Messages Across Time

Falling Through to Forever

Once Upon a Winter's Spell

(BECKONED)

Before the Storm

Twist of Fate

When the Stars Align

Once Upon a Christmas

Once in a Blue Moon

A Wish Upon a Star

(BEGUILED)

When Lightning Strikes

Storm of Time

Midnight Storm

When the Moon Falls

Stormborn Angel

(SPELLED)

Time Tempest

The Heart Remembers

A Moment in Time

Moonlight Shadows

HISTORICAL

(TAPESTRY OF BLUE AND GRAY)

Shadows Beneath Magnolia Blooms

Secrets Among Southern Roses

(IT HAPPENED BY ACCIDENT)

Accidentally Alluring

Accidentally Married

(SOUTHERN BELLE CIVIL WAR)

Beyond Enemy Lines

Love Always

Hearts Under Siege

Hearts Under Fire

Away Down South in Dixie

The Reluctant Bride

Stay with Me

Jasmine Kisses

Magnolia Kisses

Gardenia Kisses

(THE QUINNS)

Wait for Me

Take Me Home

Keep Me Safe

FATED MATES

Riley's Mate

Aiden's Mate

Brayden's Mate

STANDALONE SUSPENSE

Lost and Found

All I Want for Christmas

Serenity

Courting Alley Cat

Still Yours (Maybe)

THE ALPINE FALLS (MAYBE YOURS) SERIES

KATHRYN KALEIGH

STILL YOURS (MAYBE)
PREVIEW — YOURS FOR CHRISTMAS (MAYBE)

Still Yours (Maybe)

Chapter One

Hannah Moore

Friday Night Pizza

The Pizzeria with its fire-roasted sauce and woodfired pizza is owned and run by a second-generation family of Italians. Their parents brought their recipes with them when they moved to America from Italy, making it a unique and popular restaurant in the heart of Uptown Houston.

Italian music spills from hidden speakers blending with the sounds of the busy kitchen and the chatter of customers. Silverware and glasses clink against each other.

The tables are not those of the typical pizza parlor. The heavy tables are covered with thick white cloth tablecloths, candles in chunky white vases burning on each one.

Lush green strands of ivies wound their way up columns interspersed among the tables and over time crawled their way along the crossbeams in the ceiling, giving the indoor restaurant an almost outdoor feel.

The scent of Italian spices blends with the rich scent of pizza and the woodsmoke from the oven.

"One week from today," Olivia announces with obvious fanfare, leaning forward, her chin-length blonde-streaked hair falling forward. "You'll be married. Mrs. Theodore Smith."

Ignoring a reflexive wince, I smile brightly. Pretending a big part of that brightness isn't forced, I say the first thing that pops into my head. "I'm thinking maybe I'll keep my last name."

My two friends sitting on either side of me at the table look at me with horror in their eyes. Olivia and Madison.

Olivia is the sassy one with blonde-streaked short hair to match. Sassy is a good word to describe her. I've heard her called mouthy by a couple of people over the years. The word doesn't not fit her, but sassy is better.

Madison has long straight chestnut hair, all natural. Matches her all-business way of approaching the world. Her reading glasses do nothing to hide the beauty behind them. Serious. I'd say the best word to describe Madison is serious.

And I have shoulder-length hair in a raven-dark color, according to my stylist. If I had to sum myself up in one word, I'd have to go with complicated.

Lifting my glass of Pinot Noir with hints of cocoa, blackberry, and dark plum, I take a little sip. The red wine feels needlessly indulgent, but we're celebrating.

The three of us usually come here on Saturday nights and have a cold beer with our pizza. As Olivia sort of pointed out, I won't be here next Saturday. I'll be on my honeymoon.

Sort of honeymoon. Theo and I are combining his college football coaching conference with our honeymoon. In Tampa, Florida. What kind of fiancé would I be to say no to that? A honeymoon paid for by his college?

As he put it, that's money we can put toward a house one day. Maybe the excuse falls flat for me, but I figure it's because I'm not really a beach kind of girl. There's that and then there's the fact that his days will be spent at the conference.

I'm not for certain what I'm supposed to do all day while he's conferencing, but I'm good at figuring things out. I'll probably do some work of my own.

We use the word honeymoon loosely.

The little pizzeria in Uptown Houston is crowded as it always is. Its popularity is as much about the atmosphere as it is for the food. The food, however, is nothing to complain about. Fire roasted with handmade crust. I usually get their specialty, the margarita pizza.

The pizzeria's got that upbeat, urban vibe that people, young and old are drawn to. It's also just two blocks over from the Galleria. Far enough away that the patrons are mostly locals, but close enough that being here is still part of the happening area.

The servers may not know our names, but they recognize us. Our server tonight is John, a college student with hair too long. Claims to be a business major, but I'm not buying it. When I was a business major, and not that long ago, a guy would have been called onto the carpet for not putting forth a professional image. Maybe things are different now. Or maybe he goes to a more liberal college.

Not my problem.

"Here you go," John says. "Good hot breadsticks. Fresh out of the oven."

"Can we get some marinara sauce?" Madison asks.

"It's on its way," John says, turning just in time to see a waitress coming this way with a tray. "There it is now."

He snags the cup of marinara off her tray as she keeps walking. She says something we can't hear to John.

He just shrugs and sets the cup of marinara in front of Madison. "All good?"

"All good."

With that, he disappears into the shadows.

"I don't think that was ours," I say.

"Neither do I," Olivia agrees.

"Oh well." Madison dips her breadstick into the sauce and happily takes a bite.

The bar is currently packed, as it always is on Saturday nights. There's a line to get a table, too. And another line for takeout.

"Why would you keep your own name?" Madison asks, taking a sip of her sparkling white wine.

Just because. "Smith is such a common name," I say.

"And my MBA is in my maiden name." I shrug uncomfortably. Although keeping my name has more than crossed my mind since I agreed to marry Theo, I've never actually said it out loud.

Now, saying it out loud and getting such a negative reaction from my two best friends, I'm wondering if maybe something is wrong with the way I think.

"That's why I'm never getting married," Olivia declares definitively.

Now Madison and I look at her as though she's lost all logical thought.

"Does Dan know that?" I ask.

"Stan. His name is Stan." She bites into a crispy breadstick.

"Okay. Does Stan know that?"

"Stan doesn't need to know it," Olivia says with definite sass. "Because I'm never getting married."

Madison and I exchange a glance. That is most definitely Olivia logic at its best.

"Moving on," Olivia says. "Have you decided whether you're moving into Theo's place or if he's moving into yours?"

"We're still undecided," I say. "My place is closer to my work. His is closer to his work." I shrug. "We'll figure it out."

Madison visibly shudders. "Cutting it kind of close, don't you think? I would have needed to know this like a year ago."

"We didn't even know we were getting married a year ago."

"And that's a different topic," Madison says.

I give her a pointed look. Madison doesn't do anything that isn't on her five-ten-fifteen year spreadsheet. I've seen that spreadsheet. There is no husband on it. And yet she dates. I don't quite know why she dates when she seems to have no plan for marriage. Unlike Olivia, she just doesn't come right out and state her opposition to the institution of marriage.

The three of us had met at the Arabella, an exclusive high-rise condo building, just over three years ago. I had been a cat sitter. Olivia and Madison had been dog walkers.

We'd somehow ended up on the same elevator at the same time. Olivia and Madison had both been walking dogs and I'd been holding a cat in a carrier that I'd had to take to the vet for a client.

You would have thought that the three of us would have been fierce competitors. And yet we had too much in common to not become fast friends which soon, by way of Madison's prophetic spreadsheet, somehow morphed us into business partners.

"Are we getting the usual?" Madison asks, opening up one of the menus.

"Yes," Olivia says. "I'm up for some Hawaiian pizza."

"Hannah?"

I set my glass down. "I'm just going to have a salad."

"Since when?" Olivia asks with a vexed expression. "I thought salads were your weekday thing."

"They are," I say. "But I've got a wedding dress to fit in."

"You'll be lucky if it doesn't just drop off of you

already," Madison says. "Didn't they already tuck it in once?"

"Yes," I say. "But I can't be too careful, you know."

Olivia and Madison exchange a look.

"You're losing too much weight," Olivia says. "Order a pizza. Otherwise your dress is just going to hang there like a feed sack.

"Jitters," Madison says tell Olivia. "It's normal."

"Definitely the jitters," Olivia says.

"I don't have the jitters," I say, but it's a half-hearted protest. I've got something. I just don't think it's the jitters.

A large table nearby filled with a dozen women erupts into applause as a young lady stands up. She's wearing a white sash with the word *Bride* embroidered on it.

"Ooh," Madison says. "We should get you one of those sashes. You can wear it everywhere. All week."

"No. You should not. I wouldn't wear it."

"She's no fun," Olivia says, swirling the wine in her glass.

"We already knew that," Madison says.

I'm not even listening to them anyone.

I'm watching the activity at the front door.

Two men, handsome men, just walked in. Both of them are wearing black business suits with white button-down shirts. Nothing unusual about that.

They're striking with their suits and their expensive hair-cuts, their handsome clean-cut features (nothing unusual about that either around here), but that's not what has snagged my attention.

I know one of them. I REALLY know him.

"Hannah," Madison says, following my gaze. "Are you okay?"

I don't answer. I can't get a word out past the lump in my throat.

The man who just walked through the door is none other than Jack Thompson.

My Jack Thompson from Alpine Falls.

My husband.

Chapter Two

Hannah

Of All The Pizza Joints

Jack must have felt me staring in his direction.

It's not a small restaurant and we're not sitting near the door. We're sitting somewhere in the middle and there are people all around us. Sitting. Walking. Standing around waiting for a seat at the bar.

But he sees me.

It's like our eyes meet across the crowded room. Just like in the movies.

After saying something to his friend, a man slightly older, I don't recognize, he peels away and heads right for our table.

After my first response, freezing, my second instinct is to flee. The restroom isn't far away. I can make it before he gets here.

But being frozen in place has already won out.

Jack, his gaze never leaving mine, walks right up to our table and stops next to my chair.

"Hello Hannah," he says.

Jack is wearing a charcoal business suit with Skye Travels embroidered over the jacket pocket. His dark-colored suit and white button-down shirt are a uniform.

"Jack. What are you doing here?" I clasp my hands together in my lap.

"Of all the pizza joints, we end up in the same one. What are the odds?"

"I can't even begin to fathom."

"How are you?" he asks, his glacier blue eyes sweeping over my face. "You look well."

"I'm okay."

"I'm here with a client," he says. "So I've got to get back to it." He gaze leaves mine long enough to glance around at Madison and Olivia. "Ladies." He nods.

Then he puts a hand on my shoulder. "Good to see you Hannah."

"You too." I watch him walk away. Back to his client.

"Who was that?" Madison asks, leaning forward, her eyes wide.

"I don't know," Olivia says. "But I do know one thing. That is not Theo."

I blink and turn back to my friends as though coming out of a daze. I look from one to the other.

They both have me pinned with their gazes.

"That was Jack Thompson."

"Jack..." Olivia's eyes get huge. "THAT Jack." She turns to Madison. "Hannah was married to him."

"Get out," Madison says, looking at me now. "Married? Why didn't I know this?"

"It never came up," I say.

"It never came up," Madison says with a shake of her head. "That's the kind of thing that comes up." She looks at Olivia accusingly. "You knew."

"It came up," Olivia said in my defense.

"Well," Madison says. "As one of your two maids-of-honor. The responsible one. The one also left in the dark. I should let you know that the court is going to need a copy of your divorce papers."

"Of course," I say. "Of course they do."

"And you happen to have a copy?"

I glance at Olivia, but she's no help. Her eyes are on the menu, even though I know she knows exactly what she's going to order. "Not exactly. But I can get a copy. It's not a problem."

"Good," she says with a glance over her shoulder in Jack's direction. "Definitely not Theo."

"No," I say, shoving the hair off my face. "Definitely not Theo."

"You didn't tell me," Madison says to Olivia.

"Not mine to tell," Olivia says.

Right now I'm thinking I have one friend too many. Not that I want to ditch either one of them.

But maybe both.

Maybe I need to just ditch both of them.

But in the meantime, I've got a bigger problem.

I've got to get in touch with the clerk's office in Alpine Falls and get a copy of my divorce papers.

Maybe I thought that if I didn't tell anyone, no one would know. This is Houston. That was Colorado. It was a lifetime ago and in another world.

It was so long ago, who could possibly care about it?

I must have said that last bit out loud.

"It's all online now," Madison says. "When you go to get your license in Harris county, there's a good possibility that your social will show that you were married."

"I don't know." I hold up a hand at her expression. "But I'll get it okay? I'll get it Monday."

"Does Theo know about this?"

I slowly shake my head. "I guess he's going to find out, isn't he?"

"I don't see any way around it, Honey," Madison says.

"I'm sure it'll all be okay," Olivia says, her gaze straying over to where Jack is sitting with his client.

Of course it will.

Of course it will be.

I'm getting married one week from today.

To a perfectly nice man.

Who is most certainly not Jack.

It's been ten years since I've seen Jack Thompson.

The cute boy I'd been married to is now a handsome man. One my friends don't seem to be able to stop checking out.

Can't blame them.

I'd be the same way, but I don't dare even glance over in his direction.

Not a good idea.

Not good at all.

Chapter Three

Jack Thompson

I'd been to this Italian pizzeria once before with, actually, a different client. Very disconcerting odds since both clients, even though they don't know each other, picked the same restaurant.

That had been a few months ago, but it had not been nearly as interesting then as it is tonight.

It has the same lively urban feel to it. The same blend of Italian herbs and fire baked pizza dough filling the air.

The same Italian music mixing with the chatter of customers and the sounds of activity coming from the kitchen.

But tonight Hannah is here. Hannah, a woman I haven't seen in ten years.

The same Hannah I think about every single day.

The same Hannah I married that summer right after high school.

"I'd offer you a glass of wine," my companion, Caleb Winslow says. "But I know you won't take it."

"Bottle to throttle," I say, forcing my attention back to Caleb.

Caleb Winslow hired me to fly him from Alpine Falls to Houston. He has a meeting in the morning. Then I'm flying him back up to Alpine Falls after lunch.

I haven't been doing much flying lately. I took some time off from my job at Skye Travels to help my dad out around the ranch.

That's one of the great things about Noah Worthington, my boss. He firmly believes in both ideals and actions that family comes before all else.

When Caleb called, I jumped at the chance to get back in the cockpit. Like all pilots, at least the ones I know, I'll take any excuse for flying that I can get.

I don't mind feeding and grooming horses. Don't mind helping my dad out with any of it. I don't even mind mending fences or chopping wood or any of the other physically intensive jobs required to keep his place going.

I even rather enjoy the guided horseback tours we provide for tourists, taking them along the river and up into the back country, mostly for just a few hours at the time. Dad has always been the one leading the guided horseback rides, but with him temporarily out of commission, I've stepped in to do just about everything.

And if there's one thing I've learned over the past month or so, everything is a LOT. As a kid, working on the horse ranch, I'd known there was a lot of work involved, but since I hadn't been the one in charge, I hadn't known just how much all that work was.

Even though none of that's a problem for me, the sky still calls to me.

Sometimes I think about getting my own airplane so I can do both. Help out my dad with the family business and provide private flights.

Unless I can find someone willing to practically donate a small airplane, though, that's not something in my immediate timeline.

"So how's your dad?" Caleb asks after he orders a glass of wine for himself and I order a glass of sparkling water.

"He's still mending. The docs say he'll be out a couple of more months at best."

"But your mom is able to do some of the tours, right?"

"She can and she's quite good at it. The tourists love her. But she doesn't like leaving my dad alone. She's taking a tour in the morning, but she hired someone to come in to sit with him. Has a list of instructions a mile long."

"She's a dedicated lady. Dedicated to the business, but dedicated to your father even more. That's important."

"Hard to find," I say. My gaze is drawn back to where Hannah sits with her two friends.

I couldn't not speak to her.

I've been wanting... needing... to talk to her for years, but she vanished off the face of the earth as far as I could determine. Absolutely no social media presence. How she managed that these days, I'll never know. Seems like everybody puts their business out there for everyone to see in one form or another.

Truth is, though, I'm the same way. Other than my family's website, I don't do much on social media either. So I guess Hannah and I are kindred spirits in that way.

Unfortunately, she's having what looks like a business dinner, just as I am.

Can't very well talk to her about anything personal when she's with work associates or even friends.

At least now I have a better idea where to find her.

Houston.

Unfortunately I'm not going to be here long to find her, much less actually talk to her.

And now. Seeing her again. After all this time.

I want to talk to her all that much more.

But it's not going to happen on this trip.

Not only am I fairly certain I can't bear to go another ten years without seeing Hannah again, things have changed.

I have no choice now.

I have to find her.

Chapter Four

Hannah

Crumbling Options

"Impossible," I say, glaring at my phone.

"Meow."

Reaching down, I pick up Bandit, a little teddy bear of a cat, technically an oversized Snowshoe with thick soft fur, and hold him close against me.

I named him Bandit because of the dark patches over his eyes. He has chocolate colored ears and tail and white mittens on his feet. He has beautiful blue eyes and loves to talk. The love of talking is the Siamese in him.

"It'll be okay, right?" He purrs and rubs his face against my chin. "You're making it very hard for me to give you up, you know that, right?" He just purrs louder. "But I have to tell you, you smell like tuna."

Bandit is one of the cats I'm supposed to be putting on our website so he can be adopted. I've had him living with me for three weeks now and I still haven't posted his photo and info on the company website.

I'm surprised Madison hasn't said anything to me about it. I think she's giving me a break because of my upcoming wedding, but honestly, one has nothing to do with the other.

I just happen to like Bandit

I sit down on the sofa in my little living room and put on the brushing mitten he likes.

With papers scattered over my coffee table, it looks like a tornado came through my apartment.

Madison and Olivia are right about one thing. Theo and I have to figure out where we're going to live. Getting married in less than a week and neither one of us has made a move in either direction.

We both still have our leases and neither one of us has started packing. I'll be the first to admit, it is a bit unusual.

Right now, though, I have more important things to deal with.

While I brush Bandit, I sort through what I know.

The clerk's office in Alpine Falls doesn't have any record of my divorce. They have the marriage license. Of course. But no record of the divorce.

I called this morning. Then I called this afternoon. Got the same answer.

"I'm sorry, Mrs. Thompson. We don't see any record of

your divorce. Do you think maybe it was filed in a different county?"

What county? Seriously. Jack and I got married in Alpine Falls. We lived in Alpine Falls. We got divorced in Alpine Falls.

But Alpine Falls has not held up its end of the bargain.

Feeling my options crumpling, I Face Time Olivia.

She's at the gym running on the treadmill.

"How do you do that?" I ask.

"Do what?"

"How do you run and talk at the same time?"

"I'm in shape?" It's a statement that comes out as a question.

"Of course you are."

"What's wrong? You look vexed."

"I am vexed."

Bandit walks across my lap, turns around and walks back.

"Is that Bandit?" Olivia asks.

"No. If Madison asks you about it. No. This is definitely not Bandit."

Olivia laughs. "Don't worry. I won't tell on you."

"Good."

"Now tell me what's wrong."

"I don't know. You're in a public place."

And I can barely hear her over the roar of the treadmill and her feet pounding on the belt.

She glances left and right. Then shakes her head. "I'm wearing a headset. No one can hear you."

"Right. Well. So I called the Alpine Falls Clerk's office to get the divorce papers."

"Okay."

"They don't have them."

"What do you mean they don't have them?"

"They have no record of our divorce." I make a concerted effort to keep my voice from going full on high-pitched panic mode.

"Did you file it somewhere else?"

"That's what they suggested. No. Actually I didn't file it at all."

"Who did?"

Who did.

An innocent enough question. One I should have an answer to.

"The attorney," I say, but I've been through every piece of paper I own and I don't have a copy of it. Shouldn't I have a copy of something important like that?

"Don't panic," Olivia says. "There has to be a way to fix this."

"I've called twice now. Talked to two different people. The only two people who work there."

"You have to go there and get it yourself."

"I can't just go there and get it."

"Of course you can. It's your divorce paper. They have to give it to you."

"I don't think it's a matter of them not wanting to give it to me. I think they can't find it."

"Sometimes in those small towns like that, you have to show up to get things done."

"How do you know that?"

Olivia slows the treadmill and starts walking. It only helps me hear her a little bit better.

"I watch television. Small towns are like that."

"Well." Bandit nips at my chin. "I can't go. I can't leave Bandit."

"That's why you're not supposed to get close to the pets you're putting up for adoption."

"Try telling that to Bandit."

"You two are too far gone." She takes a drink of water from her bottle. "I think you're going to end up keeping him."

"I can't do that. I can't have a pet in my apartment."

"Oh. Right. But... Bandit's a cat... and he's in your apartment."

"Hush now. The walls might have ears."

"What about Theo's place?"

"What about it?"

"Can he have a cat?"

"I don't know." I wince. "Theo's not really into pets."

Olivia hits stop on the treadmill and picks up her phone, bringing her face closer to the phone so I can clearly see her stunned expression. "Wait. You're marrying a man who's not into pets."

I shrug.

"He does know that pet adoptions are your career, right?"

"I'm pretty sure he knows that."

"But he doesn't like pets." Oliva runs a towel over her face. "How did I not know this?"

"I guess it never came up."

"Does Madison know this?" She starts walking again.

"It's not a big deal. Theo's okay with cats as long as they're temporary."

"Oh. Well. I guess that makes it alright then." Sarcasm drips from her words.

"Maybe you can go," I say.

Olivia glares at me. "They won't give your divorce papers to me."

"Why not? It's a matter of public record."

"No. I'll be the one keeping Bandit. You need to go. They know you there. They'll give you the papers."

"You're much more intimidating."

"That is true." Using both hands, she makes a swing at her short blonde hair. "But that's not that point. You might need to sign something."

"Sign what?"

"I don't know. Maybe you'll have to get new papers."

"I don't want to talk to you anymore."

Olivia grins. "I'll shower and be over to pick up Bandit." She jabs a finger at me. "Go online and buy a plane ticket."

"With what?" I can't help thinking about my maxed out credit card.

"Get Theo to buy it."

"Have you met Theo?" I ask.

Olivia holds up her hands. "You're the one getting married to him."

"Got to go," I say. "I have things to do."

"Sometimes the truth hurts," Olivia says before she ends the call.

I hate it when Olivia is right.

But I get on my phone and start looking for a plane ticket. The first one I can afford isn't until tomorrow and it leaves at seven a.m. In the morning.

My credit card protests, but somehow goes through.

When the receipt comes in, I see why the ticket is so affordable. It's a one-way ticket to Denver.

Dropping back onto the couch, I groan.

Bandit jumps into my lap.

I wrap my arms around him. "The worst part is I have to leave you here with Olivia."

Bandit just purrs and bites at my chin.

"I'll be back before you know it."

Maybe if I say it out loud, it will manifest and come true.

Chapter Five

Jack

"You seem preoccupied," Caleb says on the flight back to Alpine Falls.

"Apologies," I say. "I guess I am. A little."

The wheels are up and I put the little jet on autopilot. It's a perfect day for flying. One of those temperate September days that promises cool fall evenings in the near future. The ones that remind me of high school football games.

Hannah and I started dating at the beginning of my sophomore year. Her freshman year.

It had been love at first sight. We'd been inseparable after that first chance meeting at the football stadium.

I'd been a quarterback and she'd been a junior varsity cheerleader.

Every memory of high school I have has Hannah in it one way or another. My freshman year either got wiped from my memory or she somehow got added in to those memories.

"Don't apologize," Caleb says. "You know you can talk to me."

"You're right." Caleb was my friend back then and we're still friends even if we don't talk. Guys are like that. We can go for years without talking. Then just pick right up where we left off. If only women were that easy.

"Well," Caleb persists.

"I saw Hannah last night."

"Hannah? Your Hannah?"

"Yes." A knot forms in my stomach. My Hannah. But not my Hannah any more.

"She's in Houston?" I nod once. "Did you know that?"

"Didn't have a clue."

He leans back, adjusting his sun glasses. "What are you going to do?"

"Nothing I can do."

"You need to talk to her."

I look over at Caleb. He's the only one who knows.

"Jack," he says. "What are you going to do?"

"Nothing," I say. Nothing has been my go-to solution when it comes to Hannah since that night.

"Okay," he says. "I guess that's worked for you so far."

"I looked for her," I say.

"Sort of."

"I did. I looked for her." We fly through a bank of white clouds making the roar of the engine seem louder somehow.

"You asked her parents where to find her." He knows good and well that I did not.

"They moved." It's been my excuse all along. No reason to change it now.

"It's been this long. Why are you so concerned about it now?"

"I've always been concerned about it," I say.

"I guess seeing her again brings up a lot of memories."

"Yeah. It does. But it's not just that."

"What then?"

I speak to the control tower in Denver and we start our initial descent.

"You're the only person who knows, right?"

"I was there," he says.

"I know you were there. I'm just asking if anyone else knows."

"Your secret is safe with me."

Caleb was there when I'd gotten the divorce papers. He'd been there as the only witness when I'd tossed them into the fire pit.

"Right." I speak to the control tower again.

"So what's different?" Caleb asks.

I look at my friend. My partner in crime. He knows enough. He might as well know the rest.

"She was wearing an engagement ring."

Chapter Six

Hannah

Winding Mountain Roads

The rental car, compliments of Madison's sky mile points is more like a go-cart in disguise than an adult car. In lime green, nonetheless.

But seeing as how I didn't have to pay for it, I'm not complaining. Not much anyway. Not out loud.

Madison scolded me for not telling her I was buying a plane ticket. Apparently she has points to share. So at least now I know how I'll be getting back to Houston.

She told me to go take care of my business, then we'll figure out how to transfer to points to a ticket for me to get home.

The drive up into mountains of Alpine Falls west of Denver is as long as I remember. I only drove this trip one time by myself and I'd been going the other direction.

The rest of the time I'd been with Jack.

Jack Thompson and I had been inseparable throughout high school.

We'd met at the first football game my freshman year and as they say, the rest is history.

We'd dated for four years and we'd gotten married in May right after my high school graduation. He'd graduated the year before me. It had been the best four years of my life.

But then Jack had left for Purdue to study aviation.

He'd put off college for a year, working on his family's horse ranch. The plan had been for us to get married, which we did, and for me to go to Purdue with him.

When that fell apart, my life had fallen apart with it. I'd had to rebuild it brick by brick.

Fortunately, my parents had moved to Denver in anticipation of my moving to Purdue. With them not living in Alpine Falls anymore, I had kept my vow to never return to Alpine Falls again.

Until now.

With every mile along the winding mountain roads, more memories come flooding back. Memories I had tucked away in the back of my mind.

Even though they're good memories, I try to keep most them at bay.

Instead, I focus on the beauty of the changing leaves. Autumn in Alpine Falls is the most beautiful time of year.

Maple trees with their red and orange leaves. Aspen trees with their golden leaves. All interspersed with a background of verdant blue spruce trees.

Winding up the hills, turning curve after curve, the forever snow-capped mountains coming closer and closer, I feel myself reconnecting with the girl I had been when I lived here.

The truth is I'm still the girl I'd left behind ten years ago.

It didn't matter that I'd gone halfway across the country and started a new life for myself. Coming back to Alpine Falls is a full on reminder of who I had been.

I'll get this thing done. Then be on my way. I glance at the time. Tomorrow. Tomorrow I'll go to the clerk's office and get a copy of the divorce papers. Then I'll head back to Denver, get on a plane, and return to Houston.

Even with the friends and family discount, my reservation at the lodge is pricey. Being part of a small start-up business, pet adoptions, is not lucrative. Especially not when I'm pretty sure I'm keeping my most profitable cat yet. Bandit. Olivia was right when she predicted that one.

I just don't know how I'm going to do it. Not with my wedding in less than a week to a man who prefers not to have a pet in the house. He knows I foster pets and he's okay with that. But a full-time cat? I don't know. I don't even know if his apartment allows pets. Mine certainly doesn't.

I pass several familiar houses telling me I'm getting closer to Alpine Falls. And apparently, over the last ten years, a lot of fancy new houses have gone up in the area. Most of them appear to hang off the side of the mountainsides. Very pretty. Very fancy.

Alpine Falls is growing.

I hadn't expected that.

I guess I expected it to always stay the small little town it always was.

Since the clerk's office is closed, I turn right and head straight to the Alpine Lodge.

The Lodge is an Alpine Falls icon. It's been here over a hundred years. Maybe one hundred fifty. And is a Christmas destination spot. People come here from all over the country at Christmastime. And, they also come here during the autumn leaf peeping season.

I pull into the little parking spot off to the side, parking as far away from the door as I can get. The little go-cart in disguise is a rental, but I still don't really want anyone to see me getting out of it.

It's a small town. People will talk. And judge. That's probably the one thing I liked least about living in a small town. The talking and the judging.

They'd talked about me and Jack getting married right after high school. I'd heard rumors that I was pregnant. I wasn't, of course, but it didn't keep people from spreading nasty rumors.

Fortunately, I'd been so blindly in love with Jack that the rumors didn't touch me. Not until they did.

But that was ancient history. I doubt anyone even remembers all that now. Enough time has passed that I'm sure they've found other people to talk about and judge.

I pull my little suitcase out of what passes for a trunk. I hadn't brought much because I'm only going to be here overnight.

Dragging it along behind me, I walk toward the lodge door.

Mr. Adams, the valet, looking decidedly older with the passing years, opens the door.

"Welcome Miss Hannah," he says, holding the door for me. "It's good to see you again."

"You too, Mr. Adams."

As I walk through the open door, he says. "I hope you're coming back to work. We missed you around here."

"Oh," I say. "I'm just here for the night."

"That's too bad. Well. Maybe you'll change your mind."

"See you later, Mr. Adams," I say, giving him a little smile.

It's a nice reminder that small towns aren't just judgy. They're friendly.

It's definitely a nice reminder.

I walk through the lobby that seems slightly smaller than it had before, back when I'd worked here as a high school senior, past the fireplace with real wood burning, open on all four sides, straight to the front desk.

"Hey Zoe," I say to the young lady, about my age, I barely recognize behind the counter.

"Oh, Hannah," she says, coming around the desk. "I saw your name on the reservation and I didn't believe it, but it really is you."

She wraps her arms around me in a big hug.

"How are you?" I ask.

She runs a hand down her stomach. "About to be a momma." She grins. "Again."

"Again?"

"My third."

"I remember when you got married."

"And I remember when you got married," she says with a big smile.

I wince.

"Oh." She puts a hand on my arm. "I'm so sorry. I still don't know what happened with you two. You were the perfect couple."

"It's complicated," I say. "And it was so very long ago. A lifetime ago."

"Not so long. Things move slower in Alpine Falls."

Great. So much for nobody remembering.

"It's good to see you," I say. "And you look happy."

"I am." She goes back behind the desk. "Let me just get you checked in."

"Right. About that. Do you think you could maybe wait until I leave to run my credit card?"

"Don't you worry about that. You used to work here. You're family. There's no charge."

"None?"

She waves a hand and keeps tapping keys. "Nope. You're all checked in. The room is available for a week, so stay as long as you like."

"Thank you, but I'm planning to leave tomorrow," I say.

"Just in case you change your mind," she says, sliding a

key across the counter. "The room is yours. Oh. And every-thing in the café is on the house. Just charge it to your room and it'll be comped."

"You can't do that," I say.

"I'll be in trouble if I don't."

"Thanks, Hannah. Thank you so much."

"Enjoy your stay."

I roll my suitcase toward the stairs.

Mr. Adams hurries over. "Let me take that up for you," he says.

I'd forgotten just how kind everyone in Alpine Falls is.

When the thing with Jack happened and I'd left, part of how I dealt with it was to put a negative sheen on everything.

Turns out that negative sheen was false.

Alpine Falls is one of the best places in the country a person could be from.

Chapter Seven

Jack

"Jack," Mother says just as I'm finishing up doing the after dinner dishes.

With my father out of commission and my mother taking care of him, not only does running the horses fall to me, but so does taking care of most of the household chores.

"The Lodge just called. Can you run three bales of hay out to them?"

"Hay? Tonight? Why?"

"When you go to the General Store and buy something do they ask you what you want it for?"

"Sometimes," I say. "Especially if it's at night. And it's something crazy like three bales of hay."

"They're having some kind of outdoor event and they need bales of hay."

"Okay. Fine." I straighten the dish cloth on the rack and run a hand through my hair. "I need to change back into my work clothes."

"Okay. But don't be too long. It sounded urgent."

Grumbling to myself, I head upstairs to change clothes and put on my work boots. "Who needs three bales of hay in the middle of the night?"

The grandfather clock chooses that instant to begin chiming the hour. Seven o'clock.

"Okay. Fine. Universe. Maybe it's not the middle of the night, but as far as needing hay bales, it may as well be."

I put on my work jeans, a flannel shirt, run a comb through my hair, then toss on a baseball cap. Wearing my work boots now, I head out to the two-story horse barn. Two dozen horses on the bottom floor. Hay on the top floor. Toss down three bales of hay onto the bed of the truck waiting below.

Still grumbling to myself, I climb into the old truck and head toward the lodge.

I'd been looking forward to an early night. A couple of hours in front of mindless television. A beer.

Work starts at daybreak at the ranch. That particular aspect still takes some getting used to.

It's a twenty minute ride out to the lodge. Everything in

Alpine Falls is twenty minutes apart maximum. Most things, like the lodge to Main Street is a five minute walk.

It just happens that the lodge and our ranch are on opposite sides of the town.

It's a drive I've made hundreds of times.

Hannah worked at the lodge her senior year of high school.

Being the overprotective boyfriend that I was, I drove her to work and I went back and picked her up after work. Every day she worked. Usually about four days a week.

I'd take her back to her house which usually added another twenty minutes onto the trip because I could never leave her without kissing on her for a while.

Those were the days.

Hannah and I had plans. Plans we never really got off the ground.

We were planning to live in Purdue while I got my degree, then come back and live with my parents for a year or two while we built a house of our own.

I was going to buy an airplane of my own and do private flights while helping out my parents at the ranch.

Funny how things turned out. I'm still thinking about getting an airplane of my own. But instead of coming back here to live, I got an apartment in Denver and went to work for Skye Travels.

An enviable job, for sure, and not easy to get. But living alone in an apartment was no life.

Since I was technically still married, albeit secretly, I didn't date. My fellow pilots could never quite figure out what was wrong with me. Probably wondered if I even liked women at all.

But as far as I was concerned, I was and still am a married man.

Unfortunately, my wife doesn't have a clue. Hannah thinks she's divorced and apparently she's engaged to someone else.

It's my responsibility to find her and tell her that she's still married before she goes through with it. I'm the one who caused us to still be married, so I'm the one who's responsible for getting us unmarried. In a timely manner.

I contemplate just how I'm going to go about that as I pull up to the lodge and park in the service area.

I put on my work gloves and drag out the first of the three bales of hay from the back of the truck.

Assuming they want the hay around back, where else would they want hay, I take off in that direction.

There's a fire in the fire pit going and several people are standing around it, some holding their hands to the warm flames. I can barely make out their faces in the moonlight. Just people in the shadows, but I can tell they're tourists.

This must be the occasion they were talking about. Whatever it is, someone deemed it worthy of having three bales of hay delivered.

I set down the first bale of hay, far enough away not to disturb the gathering of guests, and go back around for another.

After hauling the second bale of hay around and dropping it to the ground, someone coming out the back door catches my attention.

I stop. Blink.

Wonder if I'm hallucinating.

Drawn like a magnet, I take a step forward.

When she turns and looks at me, I know I'm not hallucinating.

Hannah.

Hannah, my Hannah, just walked out the back door of the Alpine Falls Lodge.

Chapter Eight

Hannah

After getting something from the café to eat, I spend all of an hour, maybe at most, in my room before I feel compelled to venture out.

Grabbing a novel from my bag, I head out. When I used to work here, my senior year of high school, I would imagine what it would be like to spend an evening in front of the fire just reading and enjoying the warmth of the flames.

The perfect opportunity to find out has presented itself.

Going down the stairs, I meet Zoe heading up with a load of towels in her arms.

"Hey," she says. "Some of the guests are having an impromptu campfire out back if you want to join them."

"Oh. Okay. I don't want to intrude on someone's private party."

"It's not private. It's a just a few random guests who wanted to get out and enjoy the cool night air. Sitting on hay bales. Having some hot apple cider."

"Hay bales?"

"Yes. Someone is dropping them off as we speak."

"Okay. Thanks. I might stop by. Nothing like fresh hay."

"Good," she says with a bright smile. "I'll see you out there."

I continue downstairs, noting that the best seats around the fireplace are taken. So maybe later. Fate, it seems, has other ideas.

I walk past the café, essentially a bar in the evenings. Big band music spilling out now. Seems some things haven't changed. Whichever manager, all family members, is on duty picks out the music so it changes from night to night and even sometimes hour by hour.

There are only a handful of customers sitting in the café/bar at the moment.

I push open the back door leading outside the lodge and stand there for a moment, savoring the crisp evening air. Compared to the Houston air, it's so clean, it almost hurts to breathe it in.

It smells like woodsmoke and blue spruce and remnants of the afternoon rainstorm.

And that's just on the surface.

It also smells like walks in the moonlight and lingering kisses.

And fresh hay.

I open my eyes and look around for the source of the unexpected scent of hay. Something I recognize from my time spent at Jack's horse ranch, not from my time spent here at the lodge.

The two memories collide in my head, repelling each other like the two north poles of magnets.

They most definitely do not go together.

But then I see why.

Two rectangle bales of hay are on the ground not far from where I'm standing.

My gaze shifts and I see the man standing next to them.

He's wearing work gloves, a flannel shirt, and a baseball cap. I instantly know that he had to be the one who brought in the hay.

The only person who would bring hay to the lodge.

Jack Thompson.

Our gazes meet and like two opposite magnetic poles, lock together.

He takes a step forward, but my own feet are frozen to the ground.

My senses, overwhelmed by the scent of woodsmoke and hay and memories of kisses... kisses by the man currently looking at me as though he just might like to be kissing me right now... have me turned inside out.

When I'd seen Jack in the Pizzeria in Houston, I'd seen

the pilot Jack. The man who belonged there in Houston. Business suit. Tie. Confident swagger.

But now I'm seeing the Jack that belongs in Alpine Falls. Flannel shirt. Baseball cap. Confident swagger.

The man carries his confident swagger with him wherever he goes, it seems.

"Of all the mountain lodges, we end up in the same one," he says. "What are the odds?"

"More likely than the same pizza joint in Houston," I say. "Everything considered."

"Yes," he says with a grin. "Everything considered."

"What are you doing here?" I ask.

He looks at me as though it's quite obvious what he's doing. "I'm dropping off hay bales."

I put a hand over my mouth to hide the bubble of laughter that threatens to spill out.

Hay bales indeed.

As though it's the most normal thing in the world.

Just dropping off some hay bales.

It was just days ago that I saw him in Houston fitting in there just as easily as he was fitting in here.

It's all in all, a bit disconcerting.

Especially since he's the person who's the very reason I'm here to begin with.

"There you are," Zoe says to Jack, coming through the door behind me. "If you would, just position those hay bales around the fire pit."

"Yes ma'am," Jack says with a little tip of his hat.

"He calls me ma'am," Zoe whispers as she passes me by. "It's so cute."

"I see," I say.

But the moment with Jack has passed and he's moving the hay bales, placing them around the fire as instructed.

"I'll be right back with the last one," he says.

When he glances over at me before he walks off, I feel that glance all the way down to my toes.

The magnetic attraction between us is most definitely still there.

Divorced or not.

Chapter Nine

Jack

As I head back to the truck to get the last bale of hay, my mind races, every instinct pushing me toward sweeping Hannah into my arms and kissing her senseless.

That's what the Jack of ten years ago would have done.

But the Jack of ten years ago would have had every reason to do so.

Hannah was my girl and then my wife.

Kissing was what we did best.

We probably did kissing better than we did anything else, talking included.

Maybe that was why we weren't married anymore.

My fix for every misunderstanding was kissing.

It seemed to work just fine.

Until it didn't.

Perhaps we'd needed to have a conversation instead that day.

But what can I say? I'd been young and besotted, drunk on her kisses, and I could never get enough. I mistakenly thought everything would fix itself.

I drag the bale of hay from the back of the truck and take my time walking back with it.

My mind is stunningly blank as I try to figure out what to say to her.

Hey Hannah. I've missed you. Oh. And by the way, we're still married.

No. That would go over like a ton of bricks.

I can't do that.

The first thing I need to do is to find out why she's here.

I know her well enough to know, however, that she isn't going to just spill her reasons to me.

No. The Hannah I know is still mad at me.

If I want her to talk to me, I've got to work my way around to it.

Get her to trust me again.

And that, I'm pretty sure, is the most impossible task I could have set for myself.

Good God. If I walked up to her right now and announced that we're still married, her trusting me would be the last I'd ever have to worry about.

It would not happen.

That's something to save for later. Something to tell her once I have a good way to explain to her exactly why we're still married.

As I settle the third hay bale around the far side of the firepit, I'm still coming up short on anything to say to her, much less how to tell her what I'm supposed to tell her.

Tourists find their way to the hay bales, using them as benches, just as was intended.

A quick scan tells me that Hannah is no longer outside.

Great. Gone just as quickly as I found her.

Fortunately, the lodge is small enough that know I can find her again. Maybe not tonight, but tomorrow.

I pull off my work gloves and stuff them in my back pocket.

Standing a moment, I debate whether to go inside the lodge to look for her or to just head back home and come back tomorrow.

The problem is I don't know why she's here and I don't know how long she'll be here.

But then the back door opens and she follows Zoe outside, both of them carrying trays of hot apple cider.

"Jack," Zoe says. "Come have some cider. You can't drive all this way over here and not sit for minute."

It would be rude to say no.

And I'm a gentleman.

So being a gentleman, I walk straight up to Hannah and take the tray of hot cider from her hands. "Let me get this for you," I say.

Looking into Hannah's verdant green eyes is worth all the cider in the world.

Priceless.

Chapter Ten

Hannah

Tastes Like Home

There's something about the smug look that crosses Zoe's features as Jack takes the tray of hot cider from me that has me perplexed.

But distracts me from that line of thinking when he sets the tray on the nearest hay bale and plucks up one of the cups of cider and hands it to me.

"You have to keep me company," he says.

I don't know any woman in her right mind who could refuse a cup of anything from Jack Thompson. Not when he's looking at me with that intense sky blue gaze of his.

He's looking at me as though there's no one else here.

It's the way he's always looked at me. Since the very first time we met at the football stadium right here in Alpine Falls.

"Thank you," I say, leaning against the bale of hay. I was supposed to be helping Zoe hand out these mugs of cider. That's what I had agreed to do when I went back inside the lodge with her.

But Zoe doesn't seem to even notice. She's doing a more than fine job of handing them out by herself.

She always has been a wonderful hostess.

In fact, she picks up one of the mugs and shoves it into Jack's hands. "Sit," she says.

Jack does as she says and sits next to me on the bale of hay.

This whole meeting with Jack almost seems orchestrated. Of course, that would be impossible. Who would do that?

"You brought hay," I say. I know we already covered that, but it seems like that's where it all begins.

"By request."

Okay. Maybe not impossible.

Just improbable.

"Do you often make late night hay bale deliveries?" I ask, taking a cautious sip of the hot cider.

"This would be the first."

"I see."

But not being one to look a gift horse in the mouth, I keep further comments to myself. Even if it was orchestrated, it doesn't really matter.

It's nice to see Jack again.

And, it suddenly occurs to me that he just might have copies of our divorce papers.

That would be convenient, wouldn't it?

But that's not something I can just come right out and ask him.

Not knowing what I know about Jack.

He would probably just grumble something and stalk off.

He's always been very sensitive about such things.

I can hear him now.

You haven't seen me in ten years and all you want from me is our divorce papers?

No. That's not a conversation I want to have with Jack.

I would much rather just enjoy the unexpected evening with him.

Besides, I'm going to the clerk's office in the morning and I'm not walking out without them. It will be one of those problem-solved situations.

"What's the occasion?" Jack asks.

"Occasion?" My first thought is that he's asking why I'm here. I haven't thought up a good answer to that particular question. Other than, of course, the truth, which I'm not ready to reveal.

"The hay bales. What's the occasion?"

"Oh. I honestly don't know. Zoe just said some guests wanted to enjoy the crisp evening air."

"It is a nice night," he says.

"Yes." It reminds me of a million evenings he and I had

spent together when we both lived in Alpine Falls. When our future stretched out before us in an endless landscape of happiness.

I swallow thickly and take another sip of my cider.

It's spicy and sweet and tastes like... home.

"It's good to see you," he says. "A pleasant surprise."

I glance over at him, my heart racing. "It's good to see you, too."

"I didn't get to talk you the other night," he says.

I look at him with a raised eyebrow. Talking was never what I would call his strong suit.

"You were with a client," I say.

He nods once.

"You're a pilot."

He nods again. "What gave me away?"

"The Skye Travels uniform for one."

"You noticed."

"Hard not to. Besides, being a pilot was your goal since, well, forever, right?"

"Yes. It was. I just don't remember working for Skye Travels ever being part of that particular goal."

I shrug. "No. But goals change and I'm thinking you talked about how much you admired Skye Travels."

"You have a really good memory," he says.

I smile. "Always."

How could he possibly think I could forget something so important to the man I dated for four years and eventually married?

But I keep that thought to myself. Maybe our relationship had a more lasting impression on me than it did on him.

"How's your cider?" he asks.

"It's good."

"Interesting."

"What's interesting?" I ask, looking over at him sideways.

"You used to hate apple cider. Wouldn't touch it."

"Yeah. Well." I hold up my mug. "Maybe I should have tried it."

"Maybe." He holds up his mug, too. "We live and learn."

Indeed we do.

Chapter Eleven

Jack

Sitting out in the chilly night air permeated with the scent of fresh hay from the hay bales I'd dropped off and the sweet and spicy scent of the apple cider in our mugs, brings back a lot of memories.

Being back in Alpine Falls is one thing to begin with, but being here at the lodge with Hannah, well, that's another thing entirely. Very unexpected and not unwelcome.

It's actually quite fortuitous, considering everything.

Considering that I happened across Hannah in Houston, saw that she's wearing an engagement ring, and then seeing her here again at the lodge.

I glance down at her hand, but she's not wearing the engagement ring she'd been wearing the other night when I saw her in Houston.

I have no doubt I saw a diamond on her finger. None.

It's the kind of thing a man notices. Especially when that man knows something she doesn't, specifically that he's still married to her.

"Tell me what's been going on with you," I say, opting to be vague and open-ended. Hoping she'll fill in some of the gaps.

"I'm part owner in a company now."

"Is that so? What company is that?"

"Forever Home Pet Placement."

"That sounds like a pet adoption agency."

"That's exactly what it is. We find pets that need a home, post them on our website, and charge a fee for placement."

I set my empty cider mug aside and stretch out my legs. "How's that going for you?"

She blows out a breath. "Interesting that you should ask."

I smile. "That bad?"

"I have this beautiful cat, a Snowshoe, that I'm supposed to be putting up for adoption, but I really want to keep him."

"You always did love cats. What's wrong with just keeping him? Surely you have more than one cat to put up for adoption."

"My apartment doesn't allow pets."

"Ouch."

"Exactly. Anyway. It's a little complicated. I just have to figure out how to keep him."

"Move back to Alpine Falls. Everyone loves animals here."

She blinks and stares at me.

I realize belatedly that that statement might be a little bit obvious, but I had actually meant it as a general suggestion.

"Right," she says. "I just can't see that happening. The two ladies you saw me having dinner with are co-owners in the company."

"You could always add a branch out here," I say.

There's that look again. The one that says she's wondering what's wrong with me.

Maybe there was a reason I was better off being the strong silent type.

"Maybe," she says, looking away and making a face when she takes another sip.

There. There's the Hannah I know and love. The girl who makes a face when she sips cider. Maybe she's learned to tolerate hot cider, but not cold cider.

"Can I take your mug?" I ask.

"Please. I see now why I didn't like it."

"I guess you just needed to try it hot."

"Maybe. So tell me what you're doing now? Are you living here in Alpine Falls?"

"Sort of," I say with a wince. "Temporarily. I'm helping my parents out at the ranch."

"So you don't actually live here?"

"No. I live in Denver. But I'll be here until my father is back on his feet."

"Is he okay?"

"Just a little accident. He's recovering nicely."

"And your mother? Is she good?"

"She watches him like a hawk. Only leaves him for trail rides when I'm not available."

"She's a devoted wife."

"How are your parents?"

She pushes the hair back off her face. "You know. We don't stay in touch. I assume that they're doing okay. If not, my brother will most likely let me know."

"I'm sorry you aren't talking to them."

"It's okay. It's just hard after what happened."

I know exactly what happened. I was there. "I feel somewhat responsible for that."

She looks into my eyes. "It's not your fault."

It's all a matter of perspective.

Here I am, feeling guilty all these years and she doesn't seem to harbor the least bit of resentment.

Maybe things aren't quite so bad as I thought they might be.

One thing is for certain. Things are better now that Hannah is back in town. Even if it is only for a moment.

Chapter Twelve

Hannah

Overdue Conversation about Things

"How long are you staying?" Jack asks.

Quiet conversations swirl around us. People just out for an evening.

Zoe brings out the makings for s'mores and there is a flurry of activity as people roast marshmallows. The scent of chargrilled marshmallows and melted chocolate is another one of those scents that brings back a flood of pleasant feelings. Not any specific memory in particular, just emotions. Reminding me how happy I was here.

"Just tonight," I say.

"Oh." Jack looks over at me. "It's a long way to come for just one night for most people."

"I'm guessing you make one night stop over flights all the time."

"I do. It's customary. But the typical person does not. Are you picking up a cat?"

"No. I had another piece of business come up." A topic I feel the need to steer him away from. "Do you know of any pets in need of adoption?"

I don't even know why I'm asking. Even if he did know of one, I could hardly take a pet back on the airplane with me.

"No," he says, with obvious amusement. "I don't know of any pets that need a home. Not at the moment anyway."

"Just as well," I say.

"I'll let you know if I come across any homeless pets."

"Okay."

"Do you want to take a walk?" he asks.

I look up at the moonlight streaming down. It is a beautiful night. "Okay," I say.

We both get up and as much as I dislike the idea of leaving the warm fire, a walk in the moonlight with Jack is worth it.

Leaving the others, we walk toward the trail leading to the river.

Already, with the conversations behind us, I can hear the rushing water up ahead.

"It sounds the same," I say, mostly to myself.

"Not much changes in Alpine Falls."

I look at him sideways. "I'm not so sure about that," I say.

"Oh? How so?"

"It seems there have been a lot of changes," I say. "The houses I saw coming in. Those weren't there before."

"Good point."

"And we don't live here," I say softly. I meant to say it mostly in jest, but instead it sounds wistful to my own ears.

I don't want to sound wistful. Not to Jack. Not when I was the one who left.

I'd had my reasons, but I'd been the one to leave nonetheless.

Maybe if Jack and I'd had a conversation, we would still be married.

We both say the same thing at the same time.

"We need to talk."

Looking at each other, we smile.

Seems we'd both had the same thought at the same time.

"You go first," he says.

"No," I say. "you."

"Okay." He shoves his hands in his pockets as we reach the river, water tumbling noisily over the rocks. "We never got a chance to talk." He pauses. A light spray of water brushes over us, evaporating as soon as it lands. "About things."

"About the text message," I say.

"Yes." He slowly blows out a breath. "The text message."

Jack had gone to Purdue to visit the campus while I

stayed behind. I was supposed to go with him, but I'd had final exams and couldn't miss. He'd had to go before the students left for the summer.

We'd talked every day and everything had seemed normal.

It was after the wedding when I saw the text message come in. Three weeks, in fact, after the wedding.

I remembered every word.

Hey. It's Rachel. So glad we got to spend some time together while you were here. Looking forward to the day you come back. XOXO

"The girl..." he says. "I don't remember her name."

"Rachel," I supply.

His brow creased, he looks at me. "Rachel," he says slowly.

I can read his mind. I know he's wondering how I could remember this girl's name after ten years.

Because I blame her for blowing up my life. I'll never forget it.

"Rachel was an academic recruiter. A sorority girl. I told her I had a fiancé, but she insisted that it didn't matter. That my life would be different at college and I'd be letting go of old relationships and making new ones."

"Was she right?" I ask.

"You left," he says, his voice soft. Strained.

Nodding, I look away, feeling hot tears burning my eyes.

He was right. I had left. I'd gone home to my parents and told them what happened.

They'd told me all sorts of things. Things they had apparently managed to keep to themselves until that point.

"You got married too young."

"Jack isn't good enough for you."

"You shouldn't trust him."

I stayed with my parents for a week.

When I finally got up the nerve to go back to the ranch where I'd been living with Jack, he was gone.

His parents tried to talk to me, but I couldn't listen. I ran back to my own parents and stayed in my room for a week.

When I finally came out, my father presented me with divorce papers.

"Just sign them," he'd said. "We'll take care of the rest. And you can go on with your life."

Eventually when I didn't hear from Jack, my parents pressuring me relentlessly, I signed.

Since I'd been accepted into the University of Houston, I headed there. I wasn't planning on going there. It was just one of those schools I'd applied to as part of my junior capstone course, been accepted to, and never declined.

So I went.

And I stayed.

The wind rustles through the trees, sending a shower of leaves falling over us.

"When I went back to your house," I say. "you weren't there."

"Where was I?"

"I don't know. Your parents tried to talk to me, but I guess I didn't listen."

"I went to your house," Jack says. "But your parents said you didn't want to see me."

I nod and turn back to him. My heart breaks for him. Like me, he still doesn't know what happened. Neither one of us knows what happened. It was like we somehow crossed paths, missing each other at every turn. And my parents.

My parents had been the worst.

He looks so young right now standing there in the shadows. Like the boy I'd fallen in love with.

"I don't think my parents wanted me to get married," I say. I expect him to laugh at that. To say that it was more than a little obvious. He'd probably known it all along, but I hadn't. I hadn't known. I'd had blinders on. Blinders that only let me see one thing. Jack.

But he doesn't laugh. When he answers, he answers with all seriousness and compassion.

"You never told me that."

"I didn't know. I didn't know until after I went home and told them about the text message. My father took things upon himself. He saw an attorney. He finally convinced me to sign." I didn't have to say what I'd signed. I couldn't bring myself to say it out loud and he knew anyway. I didn't have to say the words.

"Did you want to sign?" he asks.

"No," I say, looking into his eyes. "I didn't want to. I resisted. But my parents convinced me that it was the right thing to do. That I didn't have a choice."

"It wasn't your idea?" he asks with something that sounds like hope in his voice.

"No. I never would have done it. My father went to the attorney. He had everything drawn up. Jack... I—"

Jack's phone chimes with a message.

He pulls his phone out and looks down.

I push away the memory of finding the text message on his phone so very long ago.

Another lifetime.

It has nothing to do with now.

We're different people.

But the involuntary punch in the gut is real. The shadow of pain that lingers even after all this time is real.

"It's my mother," he says. "She needs help getting my father into bed."

"Well then." I force myself to smile and hope it comes out right side up. "You have to go."

We start walking back toward the lodge while he sends his mother a quick reply letting her know he's on the way.

"Can I see you again tomorrow?" he asks.

"I have to do... my errand, then I was going to head out."

"Driving to Denver?"

"Yes. I don't have a ticket yet, but I need to get back. My friend is cat sitting."

"Meet you at the Pizzeria? We can have lunch before you go. You have to eat."

"Okay. Sure." The Pizzeria is practically right across the street from the clerk's office.

He leaves me at the firepit and heads off toward the front

of the lodge where he'd parked. "I'll see you tomorrow," he says, giving me a broad smile.

"Tomorrow," I say, sitting down on the bale of hay.

I sit there for two seconds before I get up and head inside. Being out here is no longer interesting. Not without Jack.

Jack took the light with him.

Chapter Thirteen

Jack

I have to stop by the General Store the next morning to pick up some supplies for the ranch. It doesn't take nearly as long as I expected it to take, so I have some time to walk downtown until it's time to meet Hannah at the Pizzeria.

Quickly bored, I stop and sit on one of the benches.

I have a lot to think about and in the twelve hours or so since I'd seen Hannah, I'd gotten absolutely nothing resolved in my head.

In fact, if anything, my thoughts are more tangled than they were last night.

Last night, things had seemed so easy. Just tell her what happened. She'll understand.

But now, the more I think about it, the more I don't think it's all that easy.

She hadn't told me that she's engaged. That's a big complication.

As much as I might find myself imagining us getting back together and living happily-after-ever, I know it's not that easy.

Ten years is a long time. A lot of water has passed under our respective bridges.

Most people in our shoes wouldn't stand a chance of sorting things out and getting back together.

She and I could have had a simple conversation all those years ago and maybe we could have gotten past the misunderstanding. What Hannah doesn't know is that I'd immediately blocked the girl's number. Rachel. I really hadn't remembered her name. And what's more, I'd never seen her again.

But then our parents had gotten involved. Apparently there was no love lost between me and her parents. I hadn't known that. It's one of those things I wish I didn't know even now.

But she's engaged now to someone and our breakup had created a rift between her and her family. That's regrettable. To me family is everything. To think about Hannah not talking to her family for all these years breaks my heart for her.

I hate it that it had anything whatsoever to do with me.

I just don't know how to fix everything.

I'd say that she and I just need some time.

But then. Engaged.

I don't know how much time we have.

As I'm sitting there torturing myself with impossible thoughts, I blink and realize that Hannah is walking up the sidewalk to the clerk of court's office.

She walks with determination and purpose.

A city girl. She looks like a city girl with her long wool coat and boots that come up to her knees. A little wool cap on her head. Very chic and stylish.

My first instinct is to catch up with her. Go with her to do whatever it is she's doing.

But then I remember that we aren't a couple anymore.

That's a really hard thing for me keep in my head for some reason.

Maybe part of it is because I know we're still married.

So technically we still are a couple.

As I sit there with the cool breeze brushing against my face, it hits me like a ton of bricks what she's doing.

She's going into the clerk's office to get a copy of our divorce papers.

But she won't get them.

She won't get them because they aren't there.

She might have signed them, but I did not.

I tossed them into a fire.

The divorce papers she's looking for don't exist.

This is a problem. This is a huge problem on so many levels.

It means she really is planning on getting married again and soon. Soon enough that needs proof that she's divorced.

And it means I've got to come clean about what I did. And I've got to tell her that she and I are still married.

I get up from the bench and pace along the sidewalk, instinctively dodging tourists ambling along the sidewalk, wandering in and out of stores.

She'll come out soon enough. She'll come out empty-handed. She can't get papers that aren't there.

I feel sorry for the clerk of court and her assistant.

Hannah is going to insist that they produce papers that do not exist.

Hannah's father had left those papers with me with specific instructions to sign them and turn them in to the clerk's office.

Well. That didn't happen. That so did not happen.

I have to tell her.

Hannah deserves to know what happened.

Chapter Fourteen

Hannah

Into the Stacks

I'd always liked Mrs. Rudolph. I remembered her as a mild-mannered older lady, but now I see that she's middle-aged. Apparently people look different through the lens of a teenager. Anyone older than thirty was ancient. She still has the same kind smile, though, that I remembered.

"It's like I told you on the phone, Dear," she says. "We have a record of your marriage, but not your divorce."

I feel like I swallowed a peach pit or something equally vile and uncomfortable.

"Can I look at the records?" I ask, still daring to hope

that Olivia was right. That if I showed up, so would my divorce papers.

"Of course. It's a matter of public record. But you won't find anything."

She continues to talk as I follow her back into the rows of books. The stacks, she calls them. "You won't find anything. Besides, I'd remember if there were divorce papers for Jack. He's my nephew, you know."

I stop, my feet frozen to the floor. "What? Jack is your nephew?"

"Yes. Twice removed and all that, but still. He's family. The Thompson family has never had a divorce." She says that with so much pride that the imaginary peach pit in my stomach feels like it's going to come up.

"I didn't know he was related to you," I say, forcing myself to taking calming breaths.

"It's okay." She stops, pulls out a poster-sized book and opens it up, then puts on her reading glasses. Carefully turning the pages, she lets me look with her.

"Here," she says, pointing to an entry. "Here's your marriage. We can use these numbers to locate the actual certificate in the files." She looks a little embarrassed. "We're online now, of course, but going back and putting all the old stuff online is a bit overwhelming."

"I understand. I have a friend who does that. She's actually quite efficient at it."

"Oh? I don't suppose she's looking for a job?"

"Madison? No. She just started her own business."

"Well. That's too bad. It's hard to find someone who's good at this sort of thing and enjoys it."

"Madison lives to organize. So how far out did you look?"

"I went out a year."

"Oh." I expected her to say three months. But if she went out a year, then there's no way she missed it.

"Here. Sit on this stool. Take your time. Go as far out as you want to."

I do as she says. Then stand up and take off my coat. This is going to take awhile.

Hopefully I'll be finished in time to meet Jack for lunch. It seems like a disconnect to me. Sitting here in the clerk's office looking for a divorce notice to the very same man I'm looking forward to having lunch with.

I also feel a little bit guilty about not wearing the engagement ring I'd taken off on the flight up here. In Alpine Falls I was always Jack's girl. I might not be his girl now, but I didn't want to have to explain anything. And I didn't feel like talking about Theo.

Turns out it takes me a lot less time to scan the giant book than I expected it to. Before the hour is up, I've gone through two years, looking for our names. Just in case. And scanned part of the next before I get to the end of the book.

After looking through the first year, I don't even recognize any of the names.

Jack said things stay the same, but as someone who didn't step foot in Alpine Falls for ten years, I can most certainly disagree with that.

People come and go. Jack, even if he wasn't living here, would have heard about that from his parents. He would have kept up.

It was sort of like watching a tree grow. The person who sees the tree every day doesn't notice it, but for the person who doesn't see it for ten years, it's more than noticeable. It's almost a little bit shocking.

I close the heavy bound book, stand up, and stretch.

"Did you find anything?" Mrs. Rudolph asks, appearing at my side.

"No. I feel like I should apologize to you for doubting you."

"You don't have to apologize, Dear. I understand."

"So." I put my coat back on and watch her return the book to the stacks. "If there's no record of my divorce, what does that mean?"

Straightening, she removes her reading glasses and looks at me.

"It can only mean one thing," she says. "You're still married to Jack."

Chapter Fifteen

Jack

I stop pacing in front of the clerk's office, my hands stuffed in my coat pockets. The urge to go inside is almost overwhelming. It isn't that I want to see what she's doing.

I just quite simply want to be near her.

It's always been that way with Hannah. Since that first night I'd met her, I'd had a singular need to be near her.

Although the sunlight is warm on top of my head, the breeze is cool. Someone leaves the coffee shop and walks past with what smells like a pumpkin latte, a reminder that the holidays will be here before we know it.

The clerk's office is up a flight of six steps. I have an aunt, sort of, who runs the clerk's office. Mrs. Rudolph. She and her husband stopped by my parents' house last Christmas. A nice lady. I'm not sure she would know me if she saw me on the street.

There's no way she'd recognize Hannah. Not only does Hannah look different now, all grown up, but it's been so very long since the wedding. Hannah certainly won't recognize Mrs. Rudolph.

My mind is going in a hundred different circles, most of them connected in one way or another, when the door opens and Hannah steps out.

She's wearing a dazed expression and she just stands there, not seeing anything in front of her.

She's stunningly beautiful, my Hannah, standing there at the top of the stairs, looked all vexed and perplexed and not a little bit flushed.

Maybe she's surprised she didn't find any record of our divorce.

I'm flooded with guilt that I haven't already told her. I could have saved her the trip up here.

But then I wouldn't have gotten the chance to see her.

The wind tousles her hair and she absently swipes it out of her face.

The movement shifts her focus and she sees me standing here.

She blinks. Then tilts her head to the side and blinks again.

"Are you okay?" I ask, stepping forward. She looks a little pale. If she's going to pass out, there's no way I can catch her from here.

"I don't know," she says.

That's enough to get me moving. In two seconds, I'm up the stairs, taking her arm. "Let me help you down," I say.

She seems steady enough as I lead her down the stairs to the sidewalk below.

"Hi," I say.

"Hi."

"You were at the clerk's office," I say, pointing out the obvious.

"I... yes... I was. I didn't know Mrs. Rudolph was your aunt."

"Twice removed or something like that."

"What does that mean?" She lifts her hair and tucks it in her coat collar, something I remember her doing back when she'd tire of fighting the wind.

"I have no idea. I think it means we see her once a year. Usually on Christmas. And my mother sends her birthday cards."

A smile tugs at the corners of Hannah's lips, but it doesn't reach her eyes or turn into a full smile.

"I think we need to talk about something," she says.

"Let's talk over lunch," I say. "I've been loitering out here for too long."

"Really, Jack. You shouldn't loiter. You know that."

"I only loiter when I'm waiting for a pretty girl."

I take her hand and tuck it in the crook of my arm.

I've waited for her so many times and being together is no natural for us, she probably doesn't even think to ask how I happened to be there waiting for her at the clerk's office.

Together we walk down the sidewalk toward the pizzeria.

We have some difficult conversations ahead of us. But for just one moment in time, I can imagine that we're back in time. Walking arm in arm along the sidewalk in Alpine Falls.

Just a couple of people in love with each other.

With a bright future.

I'll take this moment in time.

Even if it is all I get.

Chapter Sixteen

Hannah

We Need to Talk

After hanging our coats on hooks next to the booth in the pizzeria, I sit across the table from Jack. A booth by the window. The table in this booth has faded stone tiles, a mountain scene painted in shades of sunset pinks.

I'm certain we've sat together in this booth before. We've sat at every booth in every restaurant in Alpine Falls.

In fact, I can't imagine there being a path or a sidewalk that he and I haven't walked together. Being inseparable in a small town for over four years will do that. The longest we were ever apart was the long weekend when he went to Purdue.

Purdue. The beginning of the end.

"Hi Jack." The young waitress stopping at our table nods in my direction. "What can I get you to drink?"

"Water for me," I say.

"Same," Jack says. "Thanks, Abigail."

"I'll be right back to take your order," Abigail says.

"She's the daughter of the football coach," Jack says as though he owes me an explanation for how he knows her.

"It's a small town," I say. "Everyone knows everyone."

"For the most part. Except, as you mentioned, for some of the new people moving in."

"You visit a lot?" I ask. "Before your father's accident?"

"Yeah. The horse ranch is a lot of work."

"What about your brother?"

"Lucas? He comes home a lot, too."

I find it interesting that Jack still calls Alpine Falls home.

"What about Trenton?"

"Trenton." Jack leans back and sighs. "Trenton is an architect in Boulder."

"An architect. I didn't see that coming."

"None of us did."

I pick up a menu and open it, but I don't see the words.

My mind is racing.

Married.

I might be still married to Jack.

According to Mrs. Rudolph, I definitely am.

I need to talk to someone. But who?

Olivia and Madison come to mind, but they would just freak out. Remind me that I'm getting married to Theo in days. Insist I do something about it. Probably even insist that I tell Theo.

I almost feel like I need to talk to my father.

He's the one who took care of the divorce. He would know which attorney he used.

But no.

The only other person I can talk to about this is sitting right in front of me.

"Here's your water," Abigail says, setting glasses of water in front of us. "Are you ready to order?"

"We'll need a few minutes," Jack says.

"Jack," I say, speaking over the lump in my throat. "I think we might have a problem."

"What kind of problem?" he asks, leaning forward, looking compassionate.

"The divorce," I say.

"That's why you're in Alpine Falls, isn't it?" he asks softly. I'm listening for it, but I don't hear any judgement in his voice.

"Yes. I need copies of the divorce papers."

His gaze flicks to my unadorned hand. I slide it under the table.

"Hannah," he says. "Is there something you need to tell me?"

I don't want to tell Jack that I'm engaged to Theo. I don't want him to know. I want Jack to see me as available. If he knows I'm engaged to Theo, then that could change everything. It could change the way Jack looks at me.

The sudden realization of just how important that feels leaves me feeling adrift.

Maybe I don't have to tell him.

Maybe I can just let him believe that I'm still available. That there's no one else.

There really wasn't ever anyone for me but Jack.

I don't want to think about Theo right now, much less talk about him.

"When I saw you in Houston," Jack says. "I thought I saw a ring on your finger."

Chapter Seventeen

Jack

Sitting in the noisy pizzeria with Hannah is like old times. I can't count the number of times Hannah and I sat right here in this booth. She used to like this booth because of the faded pink scene painted on the marble table.

Today she doesn't seem to notice it so much. She seems preoccupied. Too preoccupied to appreciate the pink painted mountain scene on the table or the actual scenic mountains in the distance.

Big band music spills from hidden speakers. Conversation swirls. Servers dart here and there, back and forth to the kitchen.

Warmth from the stone ovens in the kitchen spills out

into the restaurant along with the scent of fresh baked pizza dough.

It's taken me years to learn to voice things on my mind. I always felt like I could tell Hannah anything, but I preferred kissing to talking.

I doubt that's changed, but since kissing isn't an option right now, I have to go with conversation.

She didn't just randomly show up in Alpine Falls. She hasn't been here for ten long years. And she didn't just happen to stop in at the clerk's office for a social visit.

I saw the ring on her finger.

Sometimes the best way to get something out in the open is to just spit it out.

"I thought I saw a ring on your finger," I say.

Hannah looks like a deer in headlights.

She doesn't say anything. She just looks at me for a moment, then looks away.

"Hannah," I say. "It's okay. You can tell me anything."

She takes a deep breath and looks at me.

"I'm engaged," she says so softly I barely hear her.

The lump in my throat is unexpected. I already knew this. And yet hearing her say it out loud is like confirming one of my worst fears.

Over the years, I'd known in my head that she would be dating other men, but in my heart, I'd secretly hoped she wasn't.

I didn't date, but I had knowledge that no one else did. Well, other than Caleb. Caleb knew, but he wasn't talking.

Just because I wasn't dating didn't mean I could expect her not to.

"Are you in love with him?" I ask, dreading the answer, but needing to know.

She looks away again, but not before I see the pain in her eyes.

Seeing that pain cross her features, unleashes a whole different chain of thoughts.

Maybe she's pregnant.

Maybe she feels like she has to get married.

"I don't know," she says.

It seems like such an odd thing for her to say, I almost smile.

"You don't know," I say, forcing myself to keep a straight face. It's hard to keep a straight face when there is such unexpected joy sweeping through my system.

If she doesn't know if she loves him, then all is not lost.

"It just sort of seemed like the thing to do," she says, looking at me now with her big emerald green eyes.

"That happens."

"But Jack," she says, leaning forward and keeping her voice at a whisper. "I can't marry him. You and I are still married."

Chapter Eighteen

Jack

Abigail stops at the table and takes our order. We order a large pepperoni pizza and breadsticks.

I ask her to bring the breadsticks out first.

I selfishly want to keep Hannah here in Alpine Falls for as long as possible. And it's not just being selfish on my part. She and I have a lot to talk about.

She apparently has just discovered that we're still married.

She has no idea that I already know.

This feels like one of those times when I don't think I can win whichever way I go.

I can't lie to her and tell her I didn't know, but can I tell her that I knew?

"I know," I say.

She blinks and sits back against the booth. "What do you mean you know?"

"I mean I know. I know we're still married."

"How could you know that?" she asks, then she puts both hands on the edge of the table, squeezing so tightly her knuckles turn white. She looks a bit like she might be sick. "You wanted to get married again."

I shake my head, but she's not looking at me. She puts a hand over her eyes and looks away, biting her lip.

"Of course," she says. "You wanted to get married again, but you couldn't find me."

"Hannah," I say.

She's looking at me again. "Why didn't you just ask my parents? They would have told you where to find me. We could have figured out why the papers didn't get filed or at least how to fix it."

I'm shaking my head again. "Hannah. No." I stretch a hand out across the table and she puts her hand in mine. "I didn't want to get married again."

"Then how—?"

Abigail shows up with our breadsticks. "Here you go," she says. "Breadsticks just out of the oven." She sets them on the table between us. "And some dipping sauce for each of you." She looks from one of us to the other. "Everything okay?"

I get the feeling she's not asking about the breadsticks. Hannah tries to slide her hand back, but I keep my hold on it. "Everything looks great, Abigail," I say with a quick glance in her direction. "Thank you."

"Okay," Abigail smiles. "I'll check back. Let me know when you're ready for me to put your pizza order in."

"Will do." My gaze is already back on Hannah. I let go of her hand now and put a breadstick on one of the plates and slide it in her direction. "See if you still like these," I say.

I keep a lightness in my voice. One that seems out of place everything considered.

She breaks off a piece of breadstick, dips it into the sauce, and takes a bite.

"How could I not?" she asks. "They have the best food here."

"I think it has something to do with the elevation."

"I think you're right."

"If you didn't want to get married again?" Hannah asks after a couple of minutes. "Then how did you know?"

"Because I didn't want to be divorced."

She takes another bite. Studies me with her head tilted to the side. A sure sign that she's confused, but working something out in her head.

"I don't understand."

I fully expect all hell to break loose. But this is Hannah and she deserves to know. It's not my fault she found out before I could tell her. I still owe her an explanation about *how* it happened.

"I never signed the divorce papers."

She grows very still. I'm not even sure she's breathing.

Then she takes a deep breath as though she suddenly remembered she needs to breathe.

"My father told me he took care of the divorce."

"He did. He brought the papers to me. Told me to sign them and take them to the courthouse to be filed."

"Okay. I signed them."

"I know. But Hannah. Did you *want* to sign them?"

"No," she says. "I didn't want to. I didn't know what I was supposed to do. My parents." She looks away. "They told me it was for the best. That you weren't who I thought you were."

"You believed them."

"No. I don't know. I didn't know what to think. I was devastated."

"It's okay. Everything was chaos. And we didn't talk. We should have talked."

"We were never all that good at talking, were we?" she asks with a little smile.

That smile is something I needed to see.

"No." I smile back. "We were better at other things."

The blush that blooms on her cheeks is one of the most lovely things I've ever seen. It so reminds me of the Hannah I knew so long ago.

"But Jack," she says, leaning forward again, her hands on the edge of the marble tabletop. "What happened? How did the papers not get filed?"

"I didn't sign them. I tossed them in the fire."

Chapter Nineteen

Hannah

The Truth

"What fire?" I search his face. "You mean like literally in a fire?"

"Yes," Jack says, finishing off a breadstick as though we're having a normal conversation. "I had a fire going in the fire pit behind the house. Caleb and I'd had a beer. Maybe two."

"Wait. Caleb knows about this?"

"He was there," Jack says, sliding another breadstick onto his plate.

"Caleb knows."

"He never told anyone."

"Wait." She holds up a hand. "So for ten years... I thought we were divorced and you... You knew that we were still married."

"That just about sums it up."

"Jack," she says. "I dated. I was going to get married to someone else. Did that ever occur to you?"

"Yes. But I hoped you wouldn't."

"You can't just..." She closes her eyes. "Do you realize how crazy that is? If I hadn't seen you in Houston, my friends wouldn't have insisted I come up here and get copies of the divorce papers. I would have gotten married." I glance around feeling like I somehow committed a crime.

"I didn't know where to find you," he says.

"You knew where to find my parents," I say. "Didn't you?"

"Maybe. I'm sure I could have figured that out. I looked for you online, but I couldn't find you."

"I hate social media. And yet it's my job to put our company out there. But that's not the point. Didn't it bother you? When you dated?"

"I didn't date."

"You didn't... Wait. Never?"

"Never. I think the guys in my class thought something was wrong with me."

"I would think so."

"I couldn't date. I'm a married man."

"This is too weird," I say, pushing my plate aside, with a half-eaten breadstick on it.

"It's not that weird," Jack says.

"It's weird, Jack. It's not normal."

"I didn't want to be divorced so I didn't sign the papers." I hear some defensiveness in his voice now. But I don't care. My face feels heated and I'm having trouble wrapping my head around all this.

That I've been married for ten years and didn't know it.

Not just married, but married to the only man I ever loved. How could he let me believe that I was divorced? "Who does that?" I murmur to myself.

"Look," he says. "I'm sorry. I'm sorry this upsets you. It was never my intent to upset you."

"What was your intent, Jack? To let me go to jail for marrying someone when I was already married?"

"I don't think you would go to jail for it," he says. "It would be an honest mistake."

"A mistake. Yes. This." I sweep a hand over the table. "This is a mistake." I raise my eyes to his. "I can't do this. I have to go."

Standing up, I grab my coat from the coat hook, but I don't bother to put it on.

I start blindly toward the door, barely able to see past the tears that well in my eyes.

"Hannah," Jack calls, following me.

He catches up to me when I reach the door.

"Hannah. Wait. Let's talk about this."

"I can't, Jack." I push the door open and turn right.

I stop. I can't remember where I parked.

I don't even remember what I'm driving. Not my car.

"Hannah. Please don't leave like this."

"I have to go."

The go-cart in disguise. I'm driving the matchbox rental. Whirling around, I start walking the other way.

By the time I see my car up ahead, I realize Jack isn't following.

My hands trembling, I press the key fob and jerk the door open.

I sit in the driver's seat and lean my head against the steering wheel.

Jack stopped. He let me go.

And that hurts more than anything else.

Chapter Twenty

Jack

I have to let her go. Hannah doesn't want me to follow her, so I stop.

But I stand on the sidewalk next to a maple tree with brightly colored falling leaves right on Main Street and watch her. I watch her get into a death trap of a car and just sit there.

Every instinct urges me to follow her. To go to her.

But she made it clear she doesn't want to be near me right now. I have to respect that.

It makes no sense. She seemed understanding when she thought I didn't know we were still married.

She'd even said we could work it out. And we can.

But once she found out I knew and purposely made no effort to tell her that I sabotaged the divorce, she was no longer okay with it.

But we can't work it out if she leaves. If she leaves, there's nothing we can do.

She's leaving without what she came here for. Divorce papers.

Does that mean she won't be getting married?

If getting married to someone else makes her happy, then that's what I want her to do. But if it doesn't... then... no. I don't want her to do it.

And deep down, I know I don't want her to marry someone else for any reason.

She's my girl. Always has been.

Even if we had gotten divorced, officially, there will never be another girl for me. I'm a one girl guy.

Maybe I was waiting for her to come back. To change her mind. I knew that the divorce hadn't been her idea. I knew it was her father's doing.

That's one of the reasons, probably the main reason, I didn't go to her parents to look for her. I was pretty sure they wouldn't have told me where to find her. Why would they? They thought she was better off without me. And as far as they were concerned, she was legally divorced and rid of me.

Finally, after several minutes, she backs out of the parking space and heads toward the highway leading to Denver where she's going to catch a plane back to Houston.

I stand there until I can't see her car anymore.

An alarm goes off on my phone. I have to get back to the ranch. There's a trail ride starting soon and I'm their guide.

With my heart shattered all over again, I walk to my truck and climb inside.

There's nothing I can do right now other than let her go.

Give her time to come to her senses.

Her wedding plans will have to be delayed. She can't get a marriage license without divorce papers and she can't get divorce papers without my signature.

So unless she decides to break all the rules and go ahead with the wedding without telling anyone about me, then there's that, at least.

I can't see Hannah doing that. Hannah isn't a rule breaker.

I don't know what she'll do, but she won't get married to someone else when she's already married. She wouldn't do it even if she could get away with it.

If she'd stayed, we could have gone together to a local attorney and gotten everything signed.

Driving in the opposite direction from her, I feel my heartstrings stretching.

I don't like being away from Hannah. Never have and never will.

But I can't hold onto her like this.

It feels too much like I'm holding onto her by force.

I'm a better man than that.

With a groan of resignation and frustration, I turn the

truck around and head toward McKenna Lawson's law office.

It's a small town. Things can happen quickly if they need to.

Chapter Twenty-One

Hannah

Just Come Home

As I drive along the highway, leaving Alpine Falls, I feel like I'm leaving a part of myself behind.

Squinting against the bright sunlight, I drive along the narrow roads with other people driving too fast. People drive too fast on these narrow roads. It's not safe. Especially with me driving this little go-cart in disguise.

Deadly but beautiful.

The forever snow-capped mountains in the distance glow in the bright sunlight and here in a slightly lower elevation, I drive beneath colorful trees. Maple trees with crisp red leaves. Aspen trees with golden leaves. All interspersed with the green of blue spruce trees.

Passing by some of the fancy houses on the edge of town, woodsmoke creates a haze from the fireplaces.

Would Jack and I have built a house out here if we'd stayed together? Or would we have stayed closer to his family's ranch? I always figured we'd take over his family's ranch one day. Not that I'd been in any hurry for that to happen. It just seemed like one of those inevitable things in life.

Back then everything had seemed so easy. Back then Jack and I'd had time to kick around and do pretty much whatever we wanted to do. We'd had a good life.

Then Purdue happened. And everything fell apart.

I never should have come back here.

Olivia had been wrong. Coming here hadn't helped.

I hadn't left with divorce papers because there weren't any.

I loose cell phone service for a few miles, then as I reach Interstate 70 heading into Denver, I'm back in range.

My phone starts ringing.

A glance tells me it's Theo. Another glance tells me I have messages from both Olivia and Madison.

Had my phone not been working in Alpine Falls? Apparently not. Either that or everyone just decided to wait until now try to reach me.

I pull off at a rest area and call Theo back first.

"Hey," he says. "I've been looking for you. Where are you?"

"I had some business to take care of."

He doesn't say anything as I get out of the car and quietly close the door. The air is cold, somehow colder than it had been in Alpine Falls. Or maybe it's just me. Maybe it just feels colder because I feel like I'm going in the wrong direction.

I actually feel a little adrift right now. It's a feeling I'm not unfamiliar with. I'd just hoped that getting married to Theo would abolish that feeling once and for all.

"Olivia told me you had to go out of town."

I stop walking. Stare at the phone.

"I did." And if Olivia wasn't keeping Bandit, she and I might have words.

"You went to see your parents, didn't you?" he asks, sounding accusing.

Theo knows I'm not on speaking terms with my parents, but I hadn't told him why. Just that we didn't see eye to eye and I'd had to get away from them to make my own way.

"She wasn't supposed to tell you I went to Denver," I say.

"Hannah. Don't you think *you* should have told me? I would have gone with you."

"I haven't even seen them," I say, telling him the truth.

"Why not?"

"I'm still working up to it." It's not a complete lie.

"Okay," he says. "I know this must be stressful for you. Take all the time you need. But Hannah?"

"Yes?"

"Let me know if they're going to be coming to the wedding. You know I don't like surprises."

"Of course," I say. "But I don't think that's going to happen."

"Good. We'd have to make adjustments to accommodate them."

I can't help but compare his reaction to a possible reconciliation with my parents to Jack's. My parents had wronged Jack and yet he'd seemed genuinely sorry that I wasn't talking to them.

"I have to go," I say.

"Okay. Call me when you get home."

I disconnect the line and walk to the restroom.

Theo doesn't want my parents to come to our wedding because we'd have to make accommodations. And yet we haven't even agreed on where we're going to live after we're married. Less than one week away.

If he knew I'm planning on keeping Bandit, he'd probably blow a gasket.

And to think that I'm going to marry this man.

Was going to marry this man.

It occurs to me as I head back out to my car that I have to postpone the wedding. I can't get a marriage license without divorce papers.

With the wind blowing through my hair as I stand next to my car, I call Olivia.

"Hey," I say. "How's Bandit?"

"Hey to you, too. Bandit is fine and I'm fine, too. Thanks for asking."

I don't answer.

"What's wrong?" she asks, her voice serious now.

"I can't get married."

"You didn't get the divorce papers."

"Nope. They apparently don't exist."

"Thank goodness. Theo has been hounding me about where you are and what you're doing. You know I support you in anything you do, but Hannah. Maybe you should take another look at Theo."

"Don't worry," I say. "I'm pretty sure that he's going to vanish once I call off the wedding."

"You're calling it off?"

"I don't think you're supposed to sound that happy."

"I can't help it. I'd pick Bandit over Theo any day."

Biting my lip, I smile. My thoughts exactly. "I guess I'll come home."

"You don't sound super excited about it."

"I have to call Madison and see if she can arrange for me to use her points for a flight."

"I don't even know what all that entails."

"Neither do I." I look at the go-cart in disguise Madison arranged for me to drive. "Somehow I'm not too optimistic."

"Everything is going to work out," Olivia says. It always does. Just come home."

Home.

Why is it the word home evokes a memory of Alpine Falls?

It's because I just left there.

That's all. Nothing more.

Madison's call goes straight to voicemail.

I leave a message and continue my journey to Denver.

Chapter Twenty-Two

Jack

My mother is not happy with me. She'd been counting on me to be the tour guide for a ride into the mountains for a small group of tourists.

Right now, the thought of getting onto a horse and riding into the backcountry is the last thing I can imagine doing.

"Mom," I say. "Ask one of the neighbors to come and sit with Dad. What I'm doing right now is important. Long term important."

"Alright. I'll try to get someone." She still doesn't sound happy about it.

"If not, just cancel the ride."

"I can't do that," Mom says. "It's our business. People paid good money."

"Tell them there was a bear sighting."

"Jack. Maybe I need to rethink leaving the ranch to you."

"Maybe. Refund their money and give them a discount on their next ride."

"I worry about you."

"No need to worry. Just take care of it. Either way. And I'll see you soon."

"You're taking a flight, aren't you?"

I look across the desk at McKenna squinting at a document on her computer.

"I might be," I say. "It's a little scary that you know that."

"I know my son," she says on a sigh. "Just be safe."

"Always."

As I disconnect the line, McKenna removes her reading glasses and looks up at me. "Do you happen to have her social?"

I rattle it off.

"Okay," she says. "Most people getting divorced can't do that."

"We aren't most people," I say.

McKenna puts her elbows on the desk and leans toward me. "Are you sure? Are you certain there's no way to salvage this? I'm getting the sense that you really don't want this."

"I don't want it," I admit. "But it's the only way. It's the right thing to do."

McKenna is from the city. Houston, I think. There are lots of rumors surrounding how she ended up here, married to my friend Caleb Lawson. Caleb doesn't talk about it. But he doesn't have to tell me that they're happy.

I always liked McKenna. I have a good sense that if Hannah and I were together, McKenna and Hannah would be good friends.

"Okay," she says, then sends the file to the printer. She slides a printed copy of divorce papers across the desk. "Read over it. See if you want to change anything."

"I'm sure it's fine," I say, but I get comfortable in the chair and start reading from the beginning.

It's the right thing to do.

Knowing that it's the right thing to do doesn't keep it from making me feel sick to my stomach.

And it doesn't help knowing that these are divorce papers that I will actually sign, unlike the ones I tossed into the fire.

As I turn to the second page of the three page document, I see that McKenna walked off. I guess she wanted to give me some privacy and some space to take my time.

She's a good attorney, but even more importantly, she's a good person.

Caleb is a lucky man to have ended up married, really married, to the girl he loves.

But I'm doing the right thing.
I'm setting Hannah free.

Chapter Twenty-Three

Hannah

A Yankee Dime

Although I'm more than happy to be rid of the go-cart, I'm not enjoying standing in line at the airport. Getting a flight last minute, even with points, maybe especially with points, is a hassle to say the least.

After an hour, I'm beginning to think that I should have stayed in Alpine Falls until I had the whole flight thing worked out. That had been my plan and I should have stuck to it.

But I'd been so upset, I'd just rushed away from Alpine Falls as quickly as possible.

After splurging on a designer coffee, I sit at one of the little tables to wait. The young lady behind the desk tells me it could take some time. She'll call me back up when she has something. If she has something.

The concourse is crowded. A lot of people traveling from Denver to Houston. The usual. Business people. Families. A teenager traveling alone, headphones on his head. Oblivious to the world around him.

As I sit there holding my coffee, all those people blend into the background.

I'd been upset when I'd left Alpine Falls, but I hadn't been upset *at* Jack. Not exactly. I'd been more upset at the situation.

Ten years. Wasted. Ten years I could have spent with Jack.

But he let me believe we were divorced.

And now there's Theo.

Theo had checked my boxes. He'd been handsome. Successful. Let me do my own thing.

That last bit doesn't quite add up with who I really am.

When I'd been with Jack, we'd been together all the time. I didn't even know the concept of a boundary. We didn't need boundaries. We were a couple in every possible way. Hardly ever apart.

But pushing thirty-years-old had freaked me out a bit. Maybe more than a bit. When my doctor had asked if I wanted to make an appointment with the sperm donor clinic, something inside me had churned. That was the best way I could describe it.

All I heard was her telling me I was waiting too long to start a family. My aunt hadn't had children and she told me how much she regretted it. She told me she felt like she'd missed out on a big part of life by not having children.

For some reason those words stuck with me. Because she wasn't married and didn't have children, everything went to my parents when she passed away. I remember looking on in horror as they went through her things. Tossing. Donating. If something was important to my aunt, no one knew it.

It had been heartbreaking. I had a snow globe I'd gotten from her belongings, but I have no idea if she cherished it or not. I cherish it because it had belonged to her and I like to imagine that someone special gave it to her or maybe she went on a trip that she enjoyed and bought it or...

"Would you like some company?"

I look up, blinking, thinking I'm imagining things.

But Jack is standing there at my table.

"Jack. How did you get back here?"

"Being a pilot has its perks. I have clearance."

"But... Why? What are you doing here?"

"I thought you might want a ride to Houston."

I look into his beautiful blue eyes. Eyes so familiar.

I can't even say how happy I am to see him. Seeing him just makes my world brighter.

"I'm not sure I want to go to Houston," I say, surprising myself.

"Where would you like to go?" he asks, sitting down across from me in the other aluminum chair.

"I don't know." I look down at my untouched coffee. Alpine Falls is the answer, but I don't tell him that. I can't tell him that because there's nothing there for me.

I shake my head. "Everything is in Houston. I have to go there."

"Right," he says and a shadow crosses his face.

"I'm having trouble getting a flight," I say.

"I just happen to have an airplane." A little smile plays about his lips.

I spent the last of my credit card balance on this coffee. "Might be a little out of my league."

"Not when you know the pilot."

I take a sip of my coffee, finally, to give myself time to think of something witty to say.

"What's the fee?" I ask.

"A Yankee dime."

"A what?" I ask on a bubble of laughter.

"A Yankee dime. Surely you remember what that is."

"Of course I remember what it is. That's your fee? For flying me to Houston?"

"Yes. Innocent. Affordable."

I glance toward the airline counter where I have feeling I'm so not going to be getting a flight anytime today. "Okay," I say.

"Really? Okay?"

"Yes. I'm not getting out of here any other way."

"There's something I have to give you first," he says,

reaching into his jacket pocket and pulling out a packet of folded papers.

He sets them in front of me, a black pen on top of them.

"What's that?"

"It's what you came looking for."

The peach pit of dread is back in my stomach. Things had been going so well and now he goes and puts papers in front of me.

It has to be divorce papers. That's all it could possibly be.

Keeping my gaze on his, I slowly unfold the papers.

When I look down, I think I'm going to be sick.

It's exactly what I thought it was going to be.

Divorce papers.

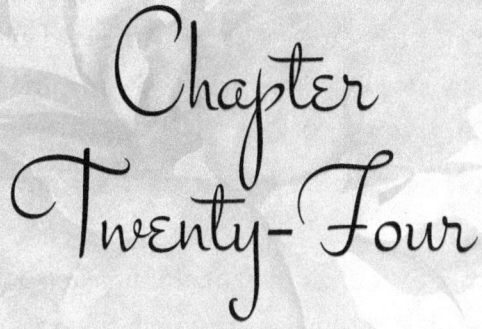

Chapter Twenty-Four

Jack

"You tracked me down to give me divorce papers?" Hannah asks, her voice barely above a whisper, her gaze locked on mine.

Her hands are in her lap now, the papers lying there as though she can't stand to touch them.

"Yes." I feel like I should say more, but the lump in my throat is keeping me from saying much of anything at all. I swallow, needing the silence to go away. "Caleb's wife is an attorney."

She looks away then, her eyes welling with tears.

I should know her well enough to know if they're tears of joy or tears of unhappiness. But I don't. I don't know.

So I just sit there quietly, waiting to see what she does.

"Is this what you want?" she asks, turning back to me finally.

"This was never what I wanted," I say, my heart in my throat.

She nods and looks down at the papers as though deep in thought. But, still, she doesn't touch them.

She valiantly fights the tears that threaten to spill from her eyes. When a tear slips down her cheek, despite those efforts, she doesn't wipe it away. She doesn't even seem to notice it.

I reach across the little table and lightly wipe it away with a finger.

She bites her lip and blinks, forcing what passes as a little smile onto her lips.

"How much for a round trip?" she asks.

"A round trip? To Houston and back? Here?"

"To Houston. And back to Alpine Falls. It would require at least one overnight's stay."

I don't know what she's saying. I know what I hope she's saying, but I don't know for sure. I don't want to make assumptions. I know better than to make assumptions.

"Overnight stays are customary," I say, keeping a straight face. This sounds suspiciously similar to a conversation she and I'd had already.

"What about pets? Are pets allowed on the plane?"

"You can bring anything you want on the plane."

She slides the papers back in my direction, touching them with only one finger. "I don't think I'll be needing these," she says.

My heart swells and I'm nearly consumed with happiness.

"So let me see if I understand the terms. You want me to fly you to Houston. Pick up a cat. And fly you back to Alpine Falls."

"That about sums it up," she says, holding onto the coffee cup with both hands.

"I see." I run a hand along my chin in a show of thoughtfulness. "That might be a little different."

"Oh?" I see disappointment cross her features and she looks away again. "It's okay. I know it's a lot."

I can't stand to see that disappointment on her face, especially knowing I'm the one who put it there.

"A down payment," I say. "I'm going to need a down payment for that."

"What kind of down payment?" With her brow creased, she slides her coffee in my direction. "I have this coffee. I've barely touched it."

As though coffee was worth anything nearly as much as a Yankee dime. Poor misguided young lady.

"No. The coffee won't do unfortunately."

"I don't have a lot to offer." There's a seriousness in her tone now. And a sadness. It's almost more than I can bear to hear.

"A kiss," I say. "A kiss for down payment."

Her eyes widen and I lean forward.

"A kiss, my sweet, and I'll take you anywhere."

She leans forward, meeting me halfway, and I press my lips against hers.

The moment is as magical as that first kiss all those years ago.

The same fluttering sensation in my stomach. The same feeling that everything is right with the world and things will never be the same again. In a good way. In a future that is lovely and bright way.

That had been in a noisy, crowded football stadium.

This was in a noisy, crowded airport.

Then someone calls Hannah's name over the speaker.

"Hannah Thompson."

Leaning back, I look at her with raised eyebrows.

"Is that you?" I ask. "Hannah Thompson?"

"I sort of never changed my name on my passport." She shrugs sheepishly.

"Things are just falling into place, aren't they? Mrs. Thompson."

"Yes. Mr. Thompson. They are."

I snatch up the divorce papers and stuff them back in my pocket.

We won't be needing these. Not ever again.

Epilogue

Hannah
Three Weeks Later

Living Our Someday

The Thompson's ranch house is one of those rambling comfortable two-story mountain houses that can easily accommodate more than one generation at the time. It's an old house. With log cabin walls, but much too modern to be considered a log cabin by any means.

Although the house is nearly a century old, everything has been updated including the kitchen with the latest appliances available on the market.

The house has lots of windows, letting in natural sunlight, especially at the back of the house, floor to ceiling windows with breathtaking views of the forever snow-capped mountains surrounding the high elevation valley. There are either wood burning fireplaces or gas burning fireplaces in practically every room and even in the middle of summer, they keep them burning. Like the gas flames burning silently in the breakfast room.

I sit at the kitchen table with Jack and his parents. It's early in the morning. The sun is barely over the horizon. But it feels right to be up this early. Getting up in time to see the sunrise is one of those things too beautiful to miss. Sleeping in is not worth missing nature's splash of color across the sky.

A rooster crows outside and a dog barks. Typical sounds that come with living on a horse ranch.

Bandit sits on my lap, rubbing his face on my chin. He's adapted quite well to being here in the house and he never sets foot outside. He spends his days sleeping in the warm sunlight or exploring the big house. Mostly sleeping.

Mr. Thompson sits across from me, a newspaper spread out in front him, his crutches leaning against the table next to him. Mrs. Thompson shuffles a stack of papers. "We have a group of ten today," she says. "A larger group than I normally like to take into the back country."

"We'll handle it," Jack says, flipping eggs in a skillet. "Hannah is good with them."

"She's a natural," Mr. Thompson smiles.

"She always was," Mrs. Thompson says.

I look over at Jack. He winks at me.

My place.

I've found my place.

I'd known it was my place all along and even though I strayed from it for a while, I've found my way back.

"Have you set a date yet?" Mrs. Thompson asks.

"Christmas," Jack says. "Christmas Eve. Right?" He looks at me for confirmation.

"That's right," I say. "The most magical day of the year."

Bandit jumps down from my lap and hops into the window ledge to chitter at a bird fluttering in the marble bird bath outside.

"I didn't know he did that," I say.

"The country air agrees with him," Mr. Thompson says. "It's good to have you back."

"It's good to be back," I say.

"I don't mind grandcats," Mrs. Thompson says, reaching over and scratching Bandit's ears. "Not one bit, but we wouldn't mind some two legged grandchildren."

Jack rolls his eyes, but I just smile. Jack and I have had this conversation. We're both on board with children.

"We have to get married first," I say, feeling a little heat on my face.

"Bah," Mr. Thompson says with a wave of his hand. "The two of you have been married plenty long enough that no one's going to be doing any math."

Jack sets a plate of eggs on the table and pulls me to my feet. "See? What did I tell you? Everyone knows we're married."

I give him a dubious look, but he just smiles and kisses

me. "It's okay. We'll have our small, intimate wedding. Get our photo in the newspaper."

"I don't care about the newspaper," I say, but it's only partially true. I do actually want everyone to know that I'm Mrs. Jack Thompson. Officially and technically.

"We have our plans," Jack says, keeping me wrapped in his arms.

"Speaking of plans," Mr. Thompson says with a glance at his wife. "We don't know what you two are thinking long-term. Probably still have things to work out. But I saw that Noah Worthington has a little Cessna for sale."

With his arms wrapped loosely around me, Jack looks from me to his father.

"You don't happen to know him, do you?" Mr. Thompson asks with a straight face.

"Only if it's the same Noah Worthington I work for," Jack says.

"Right," Mr. Thompson says, feigning innocence. "Well. Anyway. Your mother and I were thinking about buying it so you can keep living here at the ranch. And fly when you want to."

I see the emotion on Jack's face. Emotion he tries to hide, but it's there.

He and I have talked about this. Long conversations late into the night. We just hadn't figured out how we were going to come up with the money.

I'm still doing a few pet adoptions from here, but it doesn't pay much more than coffee money.

"Jack," I say, then smile over at Mr. and Mrs. Thompson. "It's perfect."

"It's what we had hoped to do some day," Jack says, kissing me again.

"Someday," I say, looking into his sky blue eyes.

He pulls me close against him and I rest my cheek against his chest. "We're living our someday," he says against my ear.

"Yes, we are."

My someday with Jack is here. This very moment.

Maybe it took us some years to find our way back around to our someday, but we're living it now.

We're living our very own happily-ever-after.

THE END

Keep Reading for a preview of
Yours for Christmas...

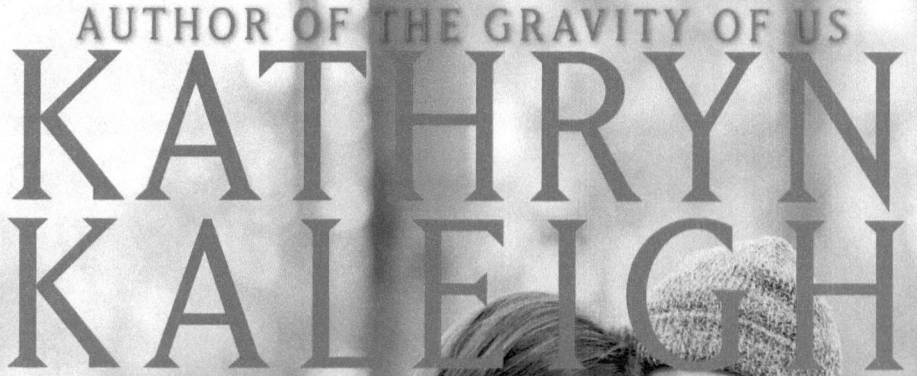

AUTHOR OF THE GRAVITY OF US

KATHRYN KALEIGH

SOMETIMES
FOREVER JUST
NEEDS A LITTLE
HOLIDAY MAGIC

Yours for Christmas
(Maybe)

THE ALPINE FALLS (MAYBE YOURS) SERIES

Yours for Christmas (Maybe)

PREVIEW

Chapter 1
Olivia Harris

"I need to confirm my reservation." I put the phone on speaker and drop it onto the bed next to my overstuffed suitcase.

Of course the automated system goes to music. Elevator music. At least it has a Christmas beat to it. So there's that.

Why did Hannah, one of my two best friends, have to get married in winter? In the mountains, no less. She could've had a wedding on a warm beach somewhere like most December brides.

Doesn't she know that packing for a cold weather trip requires ten times as many clothes?

I pull out a chunky, oversized cable sweater that's taking up a fourth of my whole suitcase and toss it aside. I'll just take it with me. I'll need something warm when I get off the airplane in Denver anyway.

At least now I have room for my maid-of-honor dress. And shoes. I almost forgot my heels.

I dash to the closet and grab the box of sparkly high heels I've only worn once. But they are a perfect match for my new burgundy evening gown with its sparkly waistband.

My dog, a little Yorkshire terrier with an adorable caramel colored head and a white body, trots into the room carrying her leash in her mouth.

She drops it at my feet and barks once.

"Hey Cupcake. Time to go outside?"

Instead of answering, she sits down and looks at me with big puppy dog eyes.

Shoving my phone, still playing nondescript music, into my back pocket, I snap her leash onto her collar and together we head to the back door of my little cottage.

Since I own the house outright after inheriting it from my grandmother, I can have as many dogs living with me as I want to.

Right now I only have Cupcake. I've taken her around to two different families for possible adoption, but they both declined. Something about her fur color not lining up.

It was their loss and since I personally think Cupcake is cute as a bug's ear, I'm keeping her for myself.

The temperature outside is warm. Currently in the seventies. Not like December at all. Cold weather is one point in favor of a mountain wedding. Christmas weather is supposed to be cold.

Cupcake runs down the steps and straight out to her favorite tree where she promptly does her business. Standing at the top of the stairs, I let the leash roll out and somehow she knows exactly when to stop before it runs out and stops. It was a one-trial learning for her to figure out just how far out she could run without her leash running out on her. She has impressive spatial skills in that way.

Not one to dilly dally, Cupcake comes bounding back up the stairs.

I pick her up and carry her the rest of the way inside. Just an excuse to bury my face in her soft fur.

When the doorbell rings, she goes on alert and wiggles until I let her down.

Not expecting anyone, I scowl at the door.

A peek outside tells me its Stan, my current boyfriend. I pick Cupcake up again so she won't run outside and open the door.

"I know," he says, holding up a hand. "I know you're leaving in the morning and don't have time for me tonight, but..." He holds up a paper sack. "I know that you forget to eat."

With a sigh, I open the door. I did forget to eat. Sort of. I got busy packing and didn't bother with it.

He smiles and kisses me on the cheek as he comes inside. "Hello Cupcake," he says to the dog in my arms.

"You're right," I say, taking the bag from him and sliding two ham sandwiches and two bags of chips out onto the table. "I didn't eat."

"Interesting music," he says.

"What? Oh." I pull my phone out of my back pocket and disconnect the call. "I was trying to confirm my reservation. I'll check online later."

"I brought Cupcake a treat." He pulls a dog treat out of his pocket and Cupcake stands up for it, then runs off to chew on it in private.

"I've decided to keep her," I say, sitting down in one of the wooden chairs at my well-worn square kitchen table that seats four.

"I know," he says.

"How do you know?"

He sits down next to me, unwraps one of the sandwiches and slides it in front of me.

"I know because you like her." He opens a bag of chips. "Besides. You need a dog."

"A pet makes a house a home," I say with a sigh. It's the tagline on our pet adoption agency website.

My two friends, Hanna (the one who ran off to Colorado and is getting married) and Madison and I have our own pet adoption agency. When we started Madison and I were handling the dogs while Hanna was handling cat adoptions.

But now that Hanna is in Colorado, we all do what we

can. Quite truthfully, Hanna isn't doing much pet adoption work at all. She lives in a tiny little mountain town and helps her husband/fiancé's family with their horse ranch. Yes. Her relationship is complicated. Long story. She was married, but thought she was divorced for ten years. So they're getting married again.

"Are you sure I can't go with you?" Stan asks.

"You've got finals to grade and two grad student dissertations to chair," I say. "And your sister is coming in from Portugal for Christmas."

"I know. I was hoping you'd be here to spend some time with her."

I smile. "Maybe later." It's about as noncommittal as I can get.

I like Stan. He's a good guy. Thoughtful. Dependable. Always thinking about me.

Is there a spark? Define spark.

He knows, should know, because I've told him, that I don't want to get married. It's not him. It's me. I like being single.

"It's okay," he says. "You need to be with your friend. Maybe my sister will be still be in country when you get back."

"Maybe," I say with a forced smile before I bite into the sandwich.

"Are you sure you don't want me to keep Cupcake for you?"

"That would be the sane thing to do. But no. Cupcake is coming with me."

"When you adopt, you go all in, don't you?"

"You know I do. That's why I try to get the dogs — and cats — out of here as soon as I can. I get attached."

He grins. I try not to roll my eyes. I know exactly what he's thinking. He's thinking that I must surely be getting attached to him by now. We've been seeing each other since spring.

It's impossible not to like Stan. It's also almost impossible to keep him from getting his hopes up that we're ever going to be something we're not.

Yours for Christmas (Maybe)

PREVIEW

Chapter 2
Olivia

Shortly after landing at the Denver airport, I discover that the car rental agencies were not prepared for the number of people heading into the mountains for the holidays.

It makes no sense to me. Hannah warned me that Alpine Falls and Whiskey Springs and a couple of the other little towns like Silver Pines, are Christmas destinations.

Every year.

If I was managing a car rental agency, I would make sure to have enough cars on hand for this time of year. Most especially enough cars to cover the reservations.

But they don't. I send Hannah a text.

> I'm in Denver. But there are no cars.

HANNAH
> Somehow not surprised.

> Options?

HANNAH
> I'll come get you.

I've already studied the map in preparation for my drive. It's a good three hour drive up to Alpine Falls. Then she'd have to drive here, then back into the mountains. At least six hours for her. Plus I have to wait here for her.

> No. Let me think.

I do a quick online search.

> I'll get a car to the train station and ride the train up there.

Thought bubbles.
Then nothing.
I shift the pet carrier on my shoulder. Cupcake is getting heavy.
I sit down on a bench and look for an Uber.

HANNAH

We have a better solution. Jack's brother is in Denver. He can swing by the airport and pick you up.

Jack's brother?

HANNAH

Trenton

So Trenton Thompson. I vaguely remember Hannah mentioning that Jack had a couple of brothers. I know absolutely nothing about them.

But. I like the idea of hitching a ride far better than I like the idea of sitting here for three plus hours waiting for Hannah to get here or worse, riding a train.

I had enough trouble with airplane staff leaving me alone about Cupcake. The thought of going through that again to try to get Cupcake on a train is daunting at best.

Speaking of Cupcake, she needs to go outside for a potty break.

Okay. I'll go outside and wait.

HANNAH

Can't you wait inside the airport?

I can. But I have to take Cupcake for a bathroom break.

HANNAH

Oh. Okay. Let me get in touch with Trenton.

I stare at the people hurrying past. Something about being in an airport makes people feel like they have to rush from one place to the next. It's part of the energy that comes with being here.

So this guy, Trenton, doesn't know he's giving me a ride.

Isn't that just great.

After I take my dog outside for a walk, I'll read up on the train. It might end up being my best option after all.

I hoist Cupcake's carrier back over my shoulder and, dragging my overstuffed suitcase along behind me, head for the nearest door to the outside world. If I ran an airport, I'd put in a park where people could walk their dogs. But, of course, that isn't going to happen.

Yours for Christmas (Maybe)

PREVIEW

Chapter 3
Trenton Thompson

My meeting went well. I'm not sure why the meeting had to be in Denver. I think the owners of the little company were trying to impress people with their fancy meeting space and city attorneys sitting at the table.

If I get the job, great. If I don't, that's okay, too.

Either way, my building design is solid and they'd be crazy to walk away from it. If they walk away, I'll use the ideas in my next projects. Sure. I'll only be able to use bits and pieces for the next client. Each client has their own unique needs.

As an architect, I pride myself on listening to what a client wants, hearing what they need, and putting it all together into something they can be proud of.

I'm back in my car before I turn my phone back on. I learned the hard way that the phone has to actually be turned off during presentations. Otherwise, even a phone on silent is a distraction.

When my father fell from a horse and had to be rushed to the hospital, I'd had my phone on silent. Keeping my focus on the presentation while watching those texts come through had been brutal. If I could rewind time, I'd probably stop my presentation and go to my family. At the time, however, I'd been determined to land the contract on the table in front of me. I'd done it, too. No one had ever suspected what I'd been going through. Fortunately it all turned out well with my father. But things could have gone badly in so many different ways.

I have a string of messages from my brother, Jack.

Jack is getting married in a couple of weeks. Married to the girl he's been secretly married to for ten years. Long story. He didn't sign the divorce papers. She thought he had.

They're doing the right thing renewing their vows in a small ceremony.

Small, but Hannah's two friends are going to be there. One of them, Olivia, is apparently already on her way here.

And she's stuck at the airport with no rental car. Typical. There are never enough rental cars.

I send my brother a message.

> Why don't you just fly down and pick her up?

My brother is a pilot with his own small jet. He literally could just fly down and fly Olivia back up to Alpine Falls.

JACK
> Because I'm out on a trail ride with eight guests.

Right. Of course. My brother Jack is running the ranch while our father is off his feet. I have a feeling that Jack and his wife are going to continue to run the ranch from here on out. Our parents are getting up in age and running a horse ranch is brutally hard work.

> Makes sense.

JACK
> Just swing by the airport and pick her up.

> I'm on the other side of town.

JACK
> She's waiting. Her name is Olivia.

> Olivia. Yes. I know. I read your other ten messages.

JACK
> Thanks Bro.

Sometimes having a family is a pain in the ass. This is exactly why I live in Boulder. It's just close enough to my family that I can visit, but I don't have to be involved in their day-to-day lives.

Living too close and things like this happens.

And apparently things like this happen anyway.

Not really having a choice about picking up Olivia from the airport, I buckle up and back out of the parking spot. I can't very well leave a young lady stranded at the airport.

Being a gentleman has been pounded into me since I was a boy. My mother raised her three boys with an iron fist and made sure we understood how to treat women.

Traffic is brutal, as always. I turn on the radio and make the best of it. Christmas music on every channel. I try not to be a scrooge, but by Thanksgiving, I'm pretty much sick of all the Christmas festivities.

As the airport comes into sight, I realize I don't know what Olivia looks like. How am I supposed to find this woman when I don't know what she looks like?

I send my brother a message, but his phone is obviously out of range.

I'm on my own on this one.

After making it to the airport, I watch as a large commercial airplane takes off practically right over the road. With my brother being a pilot, I've spent my share of time at airports, but unlike Jack, I don't have that draw to airplanes. Feeling the allure of the sky is something I can appreciate, but never share with Jack.

Instead of parking in the parking lot, I pull up to the main doors.

A woman comes out the doors, walking a little dog. The dog, a Yorkshire terrier, if I know my dogs, is rather odd looking. Cute, but odd. The woman is... actually quite stunning. She has a sassy short bob of blonde hair that just barely brushes her shoulders. She's wearing a chunky sweater over jeans and sneakers on her feet. Casual but with an urban vibe about her.

She's holding the dog's leash with one hand and pulling her suitcase with the other, a pet carrier secured to the top of the suitcase. She carries a computer bag on one shoulder and an oversized handbag on the other, balancing it all with surprising grace.

But, seriously, who brings a dog to an airport?

Since I can't leave my car, I get out and lean against the hood. Maybe someone had the good sense to send Olivia a description of me or even what kind of car I drive. Either would be helpful.

I send my brother another text.

> Would help if I had her number.

After a few minutes, the woman walks back this way, picks up her dog and sits on a bench with it in her lap. I cross my arms and keep my eyes open for someone who looks like she might be waiting for a ride.

Maybe I should just park the car and go inside to look for Olivia.

I glare at my phone.

Try sending Hannah a message, but her phone is out of range also.

Why did no one think to send me Olivia's number?

I scroll back through my previous messages, but I definitely don't have her number.

A few people come out the door, but none of them look like a woman heading to Alpine Falls. I try to imagine what a friend of Hannah's might look like.

Hannah is thin and casual-looking, but then Hannah is different because she's actually from Alpine Falls. Her friend won't be from Alpine Falls. Her friend will be from Houston.

My gaze strays back to the young lady sitting with the dog. She's also typing on her own phone and not looking too happy.

I need a sign. That's what people do in the movies.

Annoyed with myself that I didn't already think of that, I climb back in my car and write *Olivia* in big letters on a blank piece of paper.

Taking my sign, I go back to my station near the hood of the car. Now I'm feeling pretty much like a dumbass standing here holding a sign.

Jack and Hannah owe me big time.

Yours for Christmas (Maybe)

PREVIEW

Chapter 4
Olivia

> **HANNAH**
> Trenton is coming to pick you up.

I walk outside the front doors of the airport. The air out here smells like exhaust. And not only that, the air is dry. I can tell as soon as I step outside that the air is different.

Hannah told me to bring moisturizer and now I understand why.

There are cars lined up, waiting for people. Dropping people off. Typical airport.

Not seeing any grass anywhere where Cupcake can take her potty break, I find a private space with a little patch of rocks and after making sure Cupcake's harness is secure, lift her out of the carrier to do her business.

Since she was cramped up in the carrier for so long, I keep her leash short and walk around with her some, letting her get some exercise. It's not like we're going anywhere right now.

My stomach growls and I realize it's mid-afternoon and I haven't eaten anything all day. Thanks to Stan, I ate last night, so I can make it to Alpine Falls. Maybe. If I ever get there.

I sit down on a bench, happy to take from break from the weight of my computer bag and purse from my shoulders.

A man pulls up in a new sedan, gets out of his car, and leans against the hood.

He most definitely does not look like someone from Alpine Falls. Not that Jack did either when I'd seen him in Houston a few months ago.

The guy leaning on the car looks like a guy out one of those men's magazines. Perfect hair and perfect business suit. Definitely not from Alpine Falls.

Gathering Cupcake up into my lap, I send Hannah a message.

> How am I supposed to find Trenton?

No response. It doesn't even look like it's been delivered.

Great. The train is sounding better and better.

The magazine guy gets back into his car. I study the train schedules. The last train leaves in... I glance at the time... thirty minutes.

Well. So much for that. My next option is to get a hotel room and try again tomorrow.

If there still aren't any rental cars, which I am almost certain if there were no cars today when I actually had a reservation, there's no way I'll get a car tomorrow when I don't have one, I can at least get on the train. Or maybe I'm going to have to let Hannah come and pick me up after all.

Now I'm thinking crazy thoughts like maybe I should have let Stan come along. Not that Stan could have produced a rental car, but this whole ordeal would seem less daunting with someone else along.

And if I'm quite honest with myself, that's probably the main reason I keep Stan around. To have someone to do things with. Maybe it's not the best reason, but it seems like as good a reason as any all things considered in this world we live in.

Stan is dependable and safe. That's not easy to find in someone these days, at least not in my experience.

The handsome magazine guy gets out of his car and, leaning on his hood again, holds up a piece of paper. A sign?

I squint in his direction. It looks like he's holding up a sign. It's too far away, of course, for me to read it.

A sign would have been a good idea. People do that in the movies all the time. It's how strangers find each other at the airport.

It suddenly occurs to me that I need a sign. I need a sign that reads *Trenton.* That way when he drives up, he'll know I'm waiting for him.

Of course, I have no paper. An iPad, but no paper. Maybe I can make a sign on my iPad.

Or... I get up, set Cupcake on her feet, and after gathering up all my things, securing my handbag and computer bag over my shoulder, grabbing the handle of my suitcase with my other hand, and walk over to the man. If a man has a sheet of paper, he'll have more than one. It's some kind of law.

"Hi," I say, smiling at him.

"Hi." He looks a little startled that I'm talking to him.

"I'm sorry to bother you, but I was wondering if maybe I could borrow a sheet of paper."

"Okay," he says, but doesn't move.

"I'm supposed to be meeting someone, but I don't know him and I need to make a sign."

"Sure." Now he seems a little annoyed. Oh well. "Hold this." He thrusts his own sign into my hands and opens up his car door.

I glance down at the sign.

Olivia.

Keep Reading Yours for Christmas (Maybe)...

Secrets and Second Chances

Honeymoon with a Stranger

Not Our Wedding

(SILVER PINES)

The Way Back to You

Back to Where We Began

When We Were Us

(ONCE UPON FOREVER)

My Forever Guy

Our Forever Love

Forever Vows

Finding Forever

Accidentally Forever

(TRUE NORTH)

Borrowed Until Monday

Still Mine

The Moon and the Stars at Christmas

Perfectly Mismatched

On the Way to Forever

A Merry Little Christmas

On the Way Home to Christmas

It was Always You

(UNBREAK MY HEART)

Begin Again

Love Again

Falling Again

(FOR THE LOVE OF THE FLIGHT)

Just Stay

Just Chance

Just Believe

Just Us

Just Once

Just Happened

Just Maybe

Just Pretend

Just Because

(MAGNETIC NORTH)

Second Chance Kisses

Second Chance Secrets

First Time Charm

Three Broken Rules

Second Chance Destiny

Unexpected Vows

(FALLING FOR CHRISTMAS)

The Heart of Christmas

The Magic of Christmas

In a One Horse Open Sleigh

A Secret Royal Christmas

An Old Fashioned Christmas

(CITY SKYLINE BILLIONAIRES)

Billionaire's Unexpected Landing

Billionaire's Accidental Girlfriend

Billionaire's Fallen Angel

Billionaire's Secret Crush

Billionaire's Barefoot Bride

(TRULY, MADLY, DEEPLY)

The Lady in the Red Dress

On the Edge of Chance

Sealed with a Kiss

Kiss Me at Midnight

The Heart Knows

(STOLEN ECHOES)

When Cupid's Arrow Strikes

Chasing Fireflies

A Chance Encounter

(EDGE OF THE HORIZON)

The Forever Equation

Pretend Boyfriend

All our Tomorrows

Kissing for Keeps

Out of the Blue

The Princess and the Playboy

(RED LIPSTICK KISSES)

Red Lipstick Kisses and Small Town Wishes

Stolen Dances and Big City Chances

Chance Connections and Upside Down Plans

A Christmas Kiss on the Twenty-Fifth

Believe in the Magic of Christmas

Vows of Inheritance Series
(Reading Order)

Vow to Protect

Vow to Redeem

ROMANTASY

(IN THE SPIRIT OF LOVE)

Spirits of the Heart

Out of Dreams and Ashes

Etched Upon the Heart

WESTERN ROMANCE

Champagne Silver

Twilight Frost

Mountbatten Pink

(WHEN HEARTSTRINGS BECKON)

Rescued in Time

Meet me in 1879

(WHEN HEARTSTRINGS ECHO)

Messages Across Time

Falling Through to Forever

Once Upon a Winter's Spell

(BECKONED)

Before the Storm

Twist of Fate

When the Stars Align

Once Upon a Christmas

Once in a Blue Moon

A Wish Upon a Star

(BEGUILED)

When Lightning Strikes

Storm of Time

Midnight Storm

When the Moon Falls

Stormborn Angel

(SPELLED)

Time Tempest

The Heart Remembers

A Moment in Time

Moonlight Shadows

HISTORICAL

(TAPESTRY OF BLUE AND GRAY)

Shadows Beneath Magnolia Blooms

Secrets Among Southern Roses

(IT HAPPENED BY ACCIDENT)

Accidentally Alluring

Accidentally Married

(SOUTHERN BELLE CIVIL WAR)

Beyond Enemy Lines

Love Always

Hearts Under Siege

Hearts Under Fire

Away Down South in Dixie

The Reluctant Bride

Stay with Me

Jasmine Kisses

Magnolia Kisses

Gardenia Kisses

(THE QUINNS)

Wait for Me

Take Me Home

Keep Me Safe

FATED MATES

Riley's Mate

Aiden's Mate

Brayden's Mate

STANDALONE SUSPENSE

Lost and Found

All I Want for Christmas

Serenity

Courting Alley Cat

All of the books in each Series are standalone and can be read out of order. However, some books have characters from the previous stories in them.

Sign up for my NEWSLETTER to get all my romance releases, sales, Kickstarter announcements, and a **FREE** romance, SEALED WITH A KISS

www.ingramcontent.com/pod-product-compliance
Lightning Source LLC
Chambersburg PA
CBHW050302110726
47898CB00007B/2500